IN THE DEAD OF NIGHT, something awakened me—the sound of footsteps approaching my bed. And then something lunged at me. I struggled to sit up, but something thick and heavy pressed against my face. My breath clogged in my throat till my lungs would burst.

Death was only moments away. I thrashed about, my arms and legs flailing. If I allowed my head to loll back, if I surrendered to the lethargy creeping over me, my life would be snuffed out by the strong hands trying to kill me. . . .

New from Miriam Lynch

THE ROAD TO MIDNIGHT

From the moment Jennifer Graham enters the isolated castle on Midnight Mountain as companion to Adeline, the mad daughter of sinister Dr. Gabriel, she is plagued by questions that must be answered quickly if she is to leave the aptly titled *Lost House* alive.

BLACKTOWER

Miriam Lynch

BEAGLE BOOKS • NEW YORK

For my daughter, Madelaine,
with love and thanks.

Published by arrangement with the author and the
author's agent Jay Garon-Brooke Associates.

ISBN: 345-26595-5-095

First printing: May 1974

PRINTED IN THE UNITED STATES OF AMERICA

A Beagle Book

BALLANTINE BOOKS
A division of Random House, Inc.
201 East 50 Street, New York, NY 10022

CHAPTER ONE

We arrived at the gates of Blacktower in the inky darkness of near-midnight. The hack lurched to a stop and the driver climbed down from his box to the sounds of creaking wood. His face appeared palely at the window, and then the door opened.

"This is as far as I go, folks. You got to git out here."

Grandfather had dozed beside him throughout the trip from the depot. At the man's words he came awake, his eyes blinking and his mouth making the slow contortions that preceded his speech.

I was glad to leave the ill-smelling carriage and as I stepped out, I drew a long breath of salt-filled air. It stung my nostrils pleasantly; in the fetid airlessness of the swaying hack I had felt my stomach squirming.

But Grandfather hung back as we tried to help him down. He protested, "It's a good distance yet. This is only the path that leads to the house." His mind made the long journey back to the past. "I walked it many a time. Still half-a-mile to go."

"I go no further." The driver was dragging out our luggage and slapping it down on the road. "Not for a million dollars in gold would

I take a step nearer that place. For I've heered that they's strange things go on there. A quareness what people talk about though none has got the courage to see for theirsclvcs. No, siree, I keep far away from Blacktower and there's nary a soul in the village that will go near it, neither, day or night."

Grandfather made a snorting noise. "Then it's fools ye all be with your nonsense. 'Twas my boyhood home, built by my father to bring his bride into. If there's stories about it, then they were bred in the minds of ignorant, envious folk."

The driver was back on his box by the time the tirade was finished. He picked up his reins and called to his horse. The vehicle swept away from us and then became swallowed up in the darkness. And we were alone on the narrow road, five miles away from the little town of Seamount where we had left the train from Boston an hour before.

The entrance gates were monstrous and they appeared to be locked tightly. But Grandfather knew the secret of opening them, and I marveled at that freakish trick of memory when he so often forgot the simplest things.

He was an old man: I tried to keep that in mind when he behaved perversely or stubbornly, almost like a child sometimes. I had given in to him when he insisted on coming back to the house he had run away from when he was sixteen.

6

"To die," he had said. "I want to die in my old home."

I had not been able to refuse him that request, knowing sadly that death could not stand very far away from him. And I had listened as patiently as I could to his tales of the days that now, in the year of 1900, were so far in the past they seemed unreal to me. For I had not yet reached my twentieth birthday on the night I saw Blacktower for the first time; yet it is still vivid in my memory. Never shall I forget the walk up that long lane in the chill of the March wind.

Above us were ugly, tattered clouds racing across the moon. The path was rough beneath my feet and Grandfather tottered along beside me, growing weaker by the moment, I knew, yet refusing when I offered to carry his suitcase along with my own. Heavy borders of trees lined our path and stretched deep into the expanses beside it. For a while we could see nothing on either side of us nor ahead of us; and then there was a sudden flare of moonlight as the clouds ripped apart, and the house came into view.

Yes, I shall remember forever my first glimpse of Blacktower. It was enormous, a great hulk of brick and stone built on the lines of a castle. On the left of the entrance, attached to the house but seeming to stand out as an entity of its own, was the turreted tower for which the house had been named.

The uneven silhouette of its battlemented top stretched high above the roof, black against the lighter sky. There were slits of windows in it, not a glimmer of light showing in any of them. I felt a shudder sweep over me, for there was a fearsome look about that high cylinder of stone. There came into my mind thoughts of a medieval bastion, a prison where hapless humans had been banished to die. It was a strange feeling which possessed me, shrinking aversion and a nameless, unexplainable fear. Or perhaps it was a premonition. I only know that the sight of it chilled me to my bones.

I was a city girl. I was used to the busy streets of Boston, to brightness and movement and the sound of voices. In any circumstances I would have felt ill at ease and, somehow, alone. Grandfather was there beside me, true. But he had reached his allotted four-score-and-ten life years; and he had grown odd lately, slipping away from the present into a world of old memories. He talked with more and more frequency of his father, the mother he had known for only a short time, and of his sister Charlotte.

As we approached the house I saw how repulsively ugly it was. It clung there to the cliff at the edge of the sea like a giant monster. And yet it had drawn Grandfather back after fifty-five years. I heard him whisper its name in an exhausted voice, just loud enough to be audible over the subdued thunder of the surf.

We went up wide stone steps to the entrance door, a great, ornate thing with a gargoyle carved into its surface. A knocker hung from the grinning mouth and it made a loud clatter as I hit it against the wood. Then we stood for a long time in the biting wind waiting to be admitted.

Someone came at last. The woman stood with the light behind her and I could not see her features, only her slim, proudly-held body and the outline of the turban wrapped around her head.

She said, "Yes?" in a long hiss, drawing out the sibilant consonant so that it was like the sound of a snake. Her head bent as she glanced down at the suitcases at our feet. When she raised her eyes again, I could feel the stab of her gaze upon me.

"Charlotte?" Grandfather asked in a plaintive voice. "Where is my sister?"

The young woman's body continued to bar the entrance and then, finally, she stepped back and the light fell upon her face. I saw the warm, dark richness of her skin, the color of creamed coffee. She had a strange and arresting sort of beauty: long, black eyes with a jewel-like glitter in them, cheekbones sharply carved and high. Her mouth was full and lushly red and she was in the flush of her full loveliness, perhaps twenty-five or so. I was fascinated by her jewelry, a jangle of bracelets on her arms and looped gold chains at the base of her throat. And I think that I stood staring at her, for she seemed some exotic, alien creature in the bleakness of this New England setting.

Engrossed with gazing at her, I did not at first hear the flurry of sound in the hall behind her. And then a voice was crying, "Cieta, what is it? I heard the bell. At this time of night!"

The owner of the voice came rushing forward, her peignoir billowing out behind her and her little hands making nervous, fluttering motions.

"Lottie! Lottie!" Grandfather went through the door in her direction. His arms were outstretched and eager, his old face lively with happiness. "Don't you recognize me, Charlotte? It's Jasper, back home again after all these years!"

I had followed in behind him, but not too closely in order that brother and sister could have their moment of reunion alone. But Charlotte Prescott, of whom I had heard so much during the past few months, was moving back away from those reaching arms. And on her face was a look not of welcoming——as I had expected——but of something like shock and horror.

My grandaunt Charlotte should have been a female version of the Santa Claus type. She had a round little body and apple-red cheeks and a rosebud mouth. But there was nothing merry or even kindly about her in that moment. She was an old woman, only a year or so younger than Grandfather, I knew, and my first thought was that she was about to have a stroke.

Her eyes grew glassy and color suffused her face, and then it seemed to shrivel so that it looked now as though the apple had suddenly grown withered and wrinkled.

"Lottie!" Grandfather cried again, his voice faltering. "You don't know me?"

Then she spoke in a whispering way that was almost like whimpering. "Why did you come?"

I saw him sway from side to side, and I ran to him and took his arm. I could feel my eyes grow hot as I looked at the woman who was my only other relative in the world.

What I saw in that little plump face was naked fear. But I was too concerned with Grandfather's feeling to wonder or care about hers. "We have come a long way," I said indignantly. "And we sent you a letter to tell you that we were coming. If you did not want us here you should have let us know!"

She had long gray braids of hair hanging over her shoulders and when she shook her head they danced from side to side. "I received no letters. I have not heard from my brother in many years."

I was certain that she was lying. I had mailed the letter myself, taken it to the post office in a special errand, since the dispatching of it had seemed so important to Grandfather. With his weight against me, I grew bolder.

11

"He has the right to be here, hasn't he? According to his father's will, the house is half his. Just because he has made no claim on it nor returned to it for so long doesn't alter the facts. We are not intruders."

"Who are you?" Her voice was still quavery and her pursed mouth looked dry. "I do not know you."

Grandfather drew himself up and spoke. "This is Alicia, my son's daughter. She's a Lawson, too, like you and me, Lottie, and she is your grandniece. Have you no welcome for her?"

She neither answered him nor looked at him. Her gaze was still on me but I doubted if she really saw me, for her eyes had the look of little glass marbles thrust uselessly into her face. I would not have been, at any rate, an imposing figure. I did not have the proud, regal carriage so fashionable then. My bones were small and delicate; I was short of stature, as all the Lawsons had ever been; and while there were times when I knew my appearance to be pleasing—for I had my mother's width of brow and good skin and hair—this was not one of them. My skirt had become bedraggled during the long walk. My shirtwaist clung to me limply under my cloak. I felt grimy and gritty and knew that my face looked pale and cold.

"We could not leave now even if we wanted to," I said to this woman whose little button-hole mouth kept pursing and falling back into place. "It is impossible. The hack driver said that there is only one train that goes through Seamount late at night on its way to Boston. It leaves the depot at half-after twelve o'clock so we would miss it if we have not already."

My words sounded almost triumphant, but it was a poor victory. Like beating a fallen horse, I thought. I saw Charlotte Prescott turn to the dark-skinned woman and wait for her to speak. "Cieta?"

Cieta had been standing motionless with her eyes upon us. Her carved features scarcely moved as she said, "The old one, he looks as though the illness is upon him. They will have to stay the night. For if he is turned out, he may die and that would be——unfortunate. To-night," she conceded. "He may remain until morning. He and the girl."

Astonishment kept me speechless. I had taken it for granted that Cieta was a servant of some sort and yet she had made the decision about our remaining, spoken with authority. I could not imagine what her position in the household could be that she was the one to say whether we would be sent away or allowed to spend the night in the house which was partly Grandfather's.

His sister merely nodded, her face turned away from us both. Nor did she speak when Cieta picked up the two suitcases and swung them up easily onto her shoulders.

I had had no opportunity, until then, to take note of our surroundings. Now I lingered for a moment and looked around. The hall was massively large and filled with all sorts of pieces of heavy furniture: sea chests and Chinese tables and beautifully-carved chairs. Doors on both sides of the hall were closed. Near the entrance one portion of the wall bulged out in a curve which stretched high into the upper reaches of the house. This, I knew, was the indoor wall of the tower which I had seen at our approach. A door was cut into it but, like all the others along the hall, it was closed and an iron bar lay over its lock.

On my way to the staircase I passed Charlotte Prescott and I hesitated for a moment, of half a mind to go back and say something to her. I wanted to tell her that I was sorry for my sharp words of a few minutes before and that I'd had no idea we would not be welcome when I succumbed to Grandfather's coaxing to take him to Blacktower. And I felt sorry for her somehow, although I could think of no reason why she should have stirred my pity.

But she had turned away and was making her way uncertainly to the back of the house, almost as though she were walking blindly. And I could sense that she wanted nothing from me, not apologies nor sympathy nor explanations. Too, I had to catch up with the others, for Grandfather was already climbing the stairs laboriously and I knew that he was the one who needed my help.

The staircase wound up and up as far as the eyes could see, the curving lines of its banisters broken only at each of its upper stories. When

14

we reached the second one Cieta was far down its corridor; I could see the flash of her long white skirt as she turned into a door. We followed her down there, through the light of a gas jet flickering inside a misty red globe, and as we came nearer to the back of the house the sound of the sea grew louder and louder.

She left us alone in two small rooms where the beds were unmade and whose only other furniture consisted of washstands and bureaus and several chairs. In spite of the vastness of the house and the lovely furnishings in the downstairs hall, these were mean little cells with only the barest of necessities in them.

I had to search in the cupboards for linens and blankets, and I moved about hastily, for Grandfather had not stirred since the moment he had sunk down into one of the chairs. He sat there in his heavy coat, slumped in exhaustion. When I went to him and helped him out of his clothing, he seemed to have no will nor even any knowledge of my ministrations.

The water in the bathroom across the hall was cold, but he did not seem to notice that either. He fairly fell into bed and I covered him up as though he were a child——as indeed he seemed to be these days. My heart smote me at the sight of him there, his form so thin it scarcely made a ridge under the covers.

I said, "Grandfather, if you need anything during the night I will be right in the next room. Be sure to call me."

He did not hear me or else did not understand, for he made no reply. By the time I had turned down his lamp he seemed to be asleep.

Our rooms were adjacent but not adjoining and it was necessary for me to go back out into the hall again to reach mine. I did not go directly into it. Cut into the wall at the end of the hall was a window which looked out over the ocean. Beyond it came the sound of the surf with its steady, insistent rhythm. I went to the window to look out, knowing that I was not ready for sleep yet. Although my bones ached with physical weariness, my mind was whirring with memories of everything that had happened during the long day just past.

And it went back and brought out the remembrance of those hours in ordered sequence: our leaving the brick house in the West End that had been our home, boarding the train in Boston, the smell of soot and steam and the scratchy feeling of the green plush seats against my back. And then our arrival at Seamount and my having to leave Grandfather to go in search of a livery stable, and the difficulty in persuading the hack driver to harness up his carriage to take us five miles out of the village. I had had to bribe him shamefully.

There had been a moment——I felt myself grow warm with the strange excitement of that moment. It had been such a little thing, nothing at all to be mooning about when I should have been in bed. But yet it possessed me and I gave myself up to thinking about it.

We had been standing on the sidewalk in front of the livery stable waiting for the grumbling hack driver to back his rig out. And a carriage had gone down the street, slowing down when it approached us. It had stopped abreast of us and the man who was alone in it had leaned out and spoken to me.

He was young, this man abroad in the late night. The light of the street lamp was reflected in his eyes, and I saw that they were the color of bitter chocolate and that there were deep places in them, like the darkness you come upon in a lake at night. His features were sharply etched and the outthrust of his strong jaw made him look a little stern. But then he had smiled at me and his face took on a younger, brighter look; and I could only stand there staring at him like a gawking schoolgirl. I was too astounded to move or speak.

For it was a face I had never seen before and yet it was familiar to me. I had never laid eyes on this man up to that moment and yet I knew every feature as well as though I had fashioned it myself. As, indeed, I had. In my imagination.

My life with Grandfather was necessarily confined. I had devoted myself to him and so had had little time for companions of my own age. There had been few opportunities to meet and become acquainted with young men. And so, as lonely girls often do, I had woven dreams

17

of the man who would come and rescue me from my loneliness. I had seen him in my imagination as having a strong, wide-shouldered body, eyes with dark depths in them, a sternness about his face that softened only for me. I had dreamed, in short, the man who sat not two feet away from me now with reins dangling from his hands and a smile——the way I had always pictured it would be——shedding its warmth on me.

He asked, "Are you in trouble? May I help you?"

I told him that we were waiting for the hack to be brought around and he nodded. But he did not drive away immediately. We went on staring at each other and I could feel the rise of excitement within me. I was not sure what was in his gaze, whether or not it was admiration and appreciation or if I wanted so much to see those things I deluded myself that they were there.

But it was glow of interest. I knew that. It did not matter that my hair was windwhipped, my clothing rumpled from traveling. He seemed to find me good to look upon and no other man had ever gazed at me in just that way before.

Even thinking of him later could make my heart beat more rapidly. I saw his face in the blackness of the uneasy water. Then I grew conscious of the waves getting wilder and louder as the tide rose and they smashed themselves against the cliff. I felt myself shivering and the same sort of nameless fear that had gripped me at the sight of Blacktower spread over me again.

Perhaps now it was the sound of the sea which gave me this premonition of danger. I knew that there must be times when the ocean was cruel; there would have been floods, shipwrecks, people lost in its depths. Grandfather had hated so much the idea of following the sea that he had run away from home rather than accede to his father's wishes.

Yet he had returned to this place, wanting to live out his last years where there must always be the fearsome sound of the surf thunder. Hating it, he had not been able to withstand the pull of its fascination. What was the power of Blacktower and the sea beyond it that had drawn him back?

I did not want to think about puzzles like that tonight. I went back to my room and, when I was ready for bed, gave myself up shamelessly to thoughts of the man with the striking brown eyes who had smiled at me and locked his gaze with mine. For I hoped that I would dream of him. But I did not. I slept without dreaming at all for a little while.

What awakened me, in the dead of night, was the sound of footsteps approaching my bed. And then something lunged at me. Still sleep-drugged, I tried to struggle up into a sitting position. But something thick and heavy came pressing against my face. I sank back, fighting for breath which became clogged in my throat until I felt that my lungs were bursting.

CHAPTER TWO

I was suffocating and yet I had strength enough to thrash about, my arms and legs flailing. And I had wits enough to know that death was only a matter of moments away, for the pressure against my nose and mouth was growing stronger. If I allowed my head to loll back, if I surrendered to the lethargy that was creeping over me, my life would be snuffed out by the strong hands that were trying to kill me.

But I was strong, too, and the instinct for self-preservation fired me with a savagery I had never known I possessed. My hand doubled into a fist and shot up and out, and it struck against flesh. I heard a low grunt and in that instant the pressure of the soft object against my face slackened. I struggled away from it and could breathe once more. With my heart pumping as air returned to my lungs, I beat with both fists against the body of the person who stood over me. I felt the soft flesh and knew that it was a woman who was my assailant. The gurgling sound of her voice was thin and light. And then she fell back and I heard the rustle of her skirts as she fled toward the door. She had left the pillow behind. It lay beside my own, close to my head, and I shrank away from it, knowing by what a narrow margin I had escaped from being suffocated by it.

After a while I was able to get up; my legs seemed scarcely able to hold me as I went toward the door. It stood ajar and my thought was to lock it lest the woman who had attempted to murder me should come back.

I had not seen her face, only the white blur of it in the darkness as she had sprung away from me. But it must have been Cieta. Who else could it have been? I clung to the door jamb, sick with fright and the memory of my brush with death.

The house seemed to be wrapped in silence, yet it was not the quiet, peaceful kind of stillness which comes to a place when all in are asleep. It was not only what had happened to me a few minutes ago that made me feel the strange, almost unearthly atmosphere of Blacktower. As I stood looking out into that dark hall, it was as though the house were waiting for something. I felt my scalp tighten and prickle as though at some unseen danger. The dislike I had felt for this place on my first glimpse of it had sharpened into one of those strange and unexplainable premonitions which come for no apparent reason.

I told myself that I was being fanciful; frightened almost out of my wits by my narrow escape, I was allowing the darkness and the stillness to possess my mind with pictures of hidden evil. In the morning——What would I do in the morning? Face the others, Cieta and Aunt Charlotte, and pretend that nothing had happened? I was weary now, wanting only to get back to bed and lie there until daylight came.

As I was about to shut the door, I heard the faint clanging of a bell from somewhere outside the house. I stood listening, my fears pushed out of my mind for a moment as I wondered about that ringing noise. A bell buoy? But I had seen no light nor the outlines of a buoy when I had looked out the hall window. Even in the cloudy night I should have been able to see them; there had been nothing out there as far as my vision could reach except the unbroken expanse of the sea.

The clanging of the bell went on for a little while. And then it stopped completely without even an echo in the still night. It halted and was heard no more as though the buoy——if such it was——had been suddenly swept out of existence.

I was about to go back to bed, for the silence seemed even thicker now that the sound had stopped and the hall beyond my door was full of weird shadows. And my apprehension was mounting; fear was bringing a hard, cold lump to my chest. And then into the silence came other noises.

They were not very clear and at first I could not identify them, knew only that they came from beyond the window at the end of the hall, from somewhere in the vicinity of the rocky ledge which stretched down from the house to the water. What I heard sounded like footsteps, slow and uncertain, scraping against stone as though someone were climbing up over the cliff. Something seemed to draw me to that window but when I looked in its direction, I saw that there was almost complete darkness at that end of the hall with only the glass panes gleaming dully.

And then those sounds stopped, too. I went back to bed, lay there tossing and restless. Thoughts of Grandfather in the next room nagged at me. I wondered if he were safe or if the same person who had invaded my room had attacked him, too——perhaps successfully if an attempt had been made on his life.

I sprang out of bed and put on my bathrobe and slippers. When I reached the hall, I looked in both directions to make sure there was no one lurking about. Then I went into Grandfather's room and hurried to his bedside. He seemed to be sleeping deeply, although his breathing sounded shallow and loud. But he was alive; I breathed a little prayer of thankfulness for that. And I knew that there must be no more sleep for me for the rest of the night. I must remain awake, listening, on guard against whatever threatened us in this dark, strange place.

As I went back to shut his door, I heard something from the other end of the hall where the staircase stretched down to the first floor and up to the far reaches of the house. They were sounds so heart-chilling that I stopped there looking down the corridor. It seemed as though someone were crying out in pain or misery, their moans and sighs muffled and faint and yet unmistakable.

I moved a little way in their direction, sidling along beside the wall, for I feared that someone might be lying there sick and in need of assistance. There was only a faint glow from the red gas globe to provide light and it threw dancing shadows in my path. There were closed doors on either side of me, but the sounds did not seem to be coming from behind them. The moaning and weeping grew louder as I reached the bulging wall of the tower which stretched from the first floor up as far as I could see.

This was where the sounds of distress——fear or pain or grief——were coming from. I heard the weeping and the sobbing sighs. And I could not endure it. I felt as though waves of suffering were flowing out through that bulging wall and clutching at my soul. Now I no longer shivered from the cold and dark of the house, but from shattering empathic emotions.

With my teeth clenched to keep them from chattering, I fled back to Grandfather's room. Then, afraid that my presence would disturb him, I returned to my bed. I had hoped to exorcise my terror and the reflection of those terrible feelings by burrowing under the coverlet. It was useless and long before it was light, I was washed and dressed and pacing restlessly up and down.

Before I returned to Grandfather once more, I went to the hall window and looked out. The sky was gray, the sun hidden behind great masses of clouds; the sea was stormy and whitecaps rode and tossed on it. But I could see a long expanse of it and there was nothing in sight, no buoy, nothing at all that would account for the clanging bell I had heard. All that happened during the night came back in a dark memory: my struggle for life, the noises from the cliff, the sounds I had heard in the tower.

All this, I knew, I must keep from Grandfather and I fastened a smile on my face as I bent over him. "How do you feel this morning?" He did not stir as I spoke and he looked as though he had not stirred at all since I had helped him into bed.

I saw now the unnatural pallor of his face. It was almost as white as the pillow behind him, and the sight of it shocked and frightened me. In that instant I was certain that he was dead, for he lay with his mouth partly open and I could see no rise and fall of the bedclothes to show that he was breathing.

Then I reached for his hand and put my fingers on his pulse, and I felt a weak, uneven beating. Relief washed over me and was gone almost immediately because he did not move at my touch.

I cried, "Grandfather!" and lifted him from his pillow. That awakened him. He stared at me with blank eyes and began to draw his breath in labored gasps. Dampness sprang out on his forehead and when I put my hand on it I found that it was both clammy and hot. I realized that he was seriously ill, that he must have medical attention immediately.

For only a moment or two I remained at his side trying to make him comfortable. Then I hurried out of the room and down to the hall. The gas globe was dark now, its color more vividly red in the daylight. The patterns of the black, ornate woodwork and maroon wallpaper were faint in the half-light that came from the hall windows.

But even now, in the morning when the dark shadows of night were gone, there was this feeling of coldness and stillness. The windows were like staring eyes, the closed doors on either side of the hall seeming to hide secrets, and over everything was this atmosphere of hush and heaviness. No house I had ever been in before had had this oppressing effect upon me. It was as though Blacktower were some great ugly thing with an evil personality of its own——ugly in its hugeness and darkness, this still monster of a house. There seemed to be no brightness about it at all. Only in the staircases were there any evidences of taste and beauty. I fastened my eyes on the banister to keep them averted from the wall of the tower which frightened me even now, although no sounds came from behind it.

Beautiful the stairs might be, but they were treacherous with their sharp curves and the high polish of their steps. I made my way cautiously to the first floor, turned when I reached it and went uncertainly toward the back of the house.

There I found the kitchen. It was a great, cavernous place with long cooking tables and huge stoves. Charlotte Prescott was pouring herself a cup of coffee from a pot at one of the stoves. At a table Cieta was chopping at a plucked chicken. In one of her slender hands she held a butcher's knife, and I could not take my gaze away from that sharp, shining blade. I stood as though hypnotized, all the terrors of the past night flowing over me again. With an effort I wrenched my eyes away and looked across the room at my grandaunt.

She seemed to shrink away from my glance. Deep lines at the corners of her mouth pulled face down into an expression of bleakness; but she was impeccably dressed and I became conscious of my own careless appearance. I had not taken time to wind my hair into its usual psyche knot and my shoes were dusty from the long walk up the lane the night before. My challis morning dress still wore creases from being folded into my suitcase.

I said breathlessly, "I am sorry to be in this state of dishabille, Aunt——Aunt Charlotte." My voice stumbled over the form of address. She was not the sort of person one could call "Aunt" easily and naturally. But she was my grandfather's sister and all my pent-up emotions rushed out to her for I was desperate and desperately afraid. I blurted, "Someone tried to kill me last night!"

From the corner of my eye I saw Cieta move and the blade was a bright flash as her hand dropped. Aunt Charlotte went on staring at me, her round eyes hooded, the fleshly folds of her face settling into hardness.

"Surely you are mistaken!" Cieta's voice was smooth and sweet. "You must have dreamed this, of course. Such a thing——but perhaps you are joking?"

I cried shrilly, "It is true, I tell you! Someone came into my room——a woman. There was a pillow, she tried to smother me with a pillow. It is still there in my room!"

"One of your own, that is what it was. There are two on all the beds. And if you were in nightmare, you could have turned over, felt the pillow against your face——"

The persuasive voice went on, describing something that had not happened. She spoke with such authority, made the explanation sound so logical that for a moment I was uncertain. Then I remembered the pressure of that soft object against my nose and mouth, a reflection of the wild panic I had felt came pouring over me again. I remembered the grunting voice, the feel of soft flesh under my fist and the sound of rustling skirts as their owner fled.

I wanted to accuse her then and there but she stood staring at me proudly and she looked, somehow, invincible. A nightmare indeed! I turned to appeal to Aunt Charlotte and saw that her face had seemed to crumble. Her eyes were blank now and when she spoke it was in a whisper.

"Yes, that is the way it must have been!"

It took me a moment or two to reply. And then I said, "If you will not believe me, there is nothing I can do. I know that for some reason you do not want us here. And we will leave as soon as——" Then I realized why I had come to seek her out. "Aunt Charlotte, Grandfather is ill this morning. I shall have to ask you to call a doctor for him."

When I said "doctor" they both seemed to freeze into stillness. Charlotte Prescott stood holding her coffee cup at an awkward position. Cieta's hands, one resting on the carcass of the chicken and the other with the knife in it, might have been carved of pale brown wood. The scene was like the silly game children play, when all the participants in it are rendered motionless by the saying of a certain word.

The silence stretched until I could bear it no longer and I cried, "Didn't you understand me? Grandfather is sick and needs a physician. Will you please summon one?"

Cieta was the first to move. Her head, held high and turban-bound, turned slowly and she looked at Aunt Charlotte. I could see nothing in those black-jewel eyes, but there was about her an attitude of tenseness.

As I looked at her, waiting for someone to speak, I was struck once more by her strange, exotic beauty. And I wondered how she had happened to come to Blacktower. Even in Boston, a cosmopolitan city, she would have been conspicuous with the high, white turban and the cast of her features. I could not guess her background, but she made me think of hot, faraway places, of tropical sunshine and jungle drums.

Beautiful, yes, but there was something frightening about her too, some aura of hidden evil.

"Tell her!" she said to Aunt Charlotte. "Tell her that there will be no doctor here, now or ever!"

I said, "Please! Please, he may die!" and heard my voice crack. Aunt Charlotte turned to look at me. Her face had changed color and her little mouth was working.

"He is that sick? Jasper is seriously ill?"

I told her the condition I had found Grandfather in, and she whimpered a little. Then something inexplicable seemed to happen to her. She drew herself up and I saw her head shake back and forth.

It seemed that she was refusing my request and I stood and stared at her with my mouth hanging open. I found it impossible to believe that she would deny her own brother the services of a physician. Grandfather had so often spoken of his sister with nostalgic longing. I had received the impression that in their growing-up days they had been close and loving. But had she ever actually loved him at all?

I remembered other things I had been told about her. She had been, so Grandfather had said, a virtual slave to her father, had seldom ventured out into the world beyond Blacktower. When Grandfather had escaped Captain Lawson's tyranny by running away from home, Aunt Charlotte had been fourteen years old but was treated like a little girl of five. Possessive, domineering, strong-willed, the captain had attempted to keep both his children under his thumb. Charlotte had not rebelled.

There had been letters between Grandfather and his sister for a while. He knew that somehow she had managed to meet Thomas Prescott and become his wife, but that marriage had been short-lived and not a true one in any sense of the word. They had lived in this house where Charlotte's father must have always been the master.

And his daughter must have gone on being

subservient to the one who would not release her from his domination. Thomas Prescott, who remained only a shadowy figure to me always, had died fairly young. According to Grandfather, that death had not altered Charlotte's way of life to any degree. She had gone on being her father's precious baby girl, his handservant, his devoted nurse during his last years. He had been the great love of her life. Perhaps there had not been much feeling left over for either her husband or her brother.

And perhaps there was the fact that Jasper Lawson was little more than a stranger to her now. Or perhaps, on her father's behalf, she had never forgiven her brother for breaking the paternal bonds when he was sixteen.

But, I told myself almost frantically, she could not refuse him help now. "He may die!" I cried out. "Unless someone takes care of him right away, I am afraid——I am afraid that he will not last very long!" And I felt the hot wash of tears pour from my eyes so that the kitchen became a blur of wetness. I did not see her turn to Cieta, I could only hear her pleading voice and then I knew that she had not been denying my request but the fact of what I had told her.

"He is my brother, after all. Cieta, all the other things——I have let you go unhampered. But this, this is Jasper! I will not stand for his death! I will not!"

There was a long pause and when my vision cleared I saw that the two women stood with their eyes locked. I was surprised that my grandaunt would speak so defiantly; until now she had seemed like Cieta's shadow, Cieta's echo. But at last she seemed like the mistress giving the orders to the servant.

Cieta's head bowed in a way that seemed mocking. She said, "Perhaps it is best. We must keep him alive, must we not?" And then she added softly, "For now."

She moved in the direction of the door. "Perhaps I shall go to see for myself." Her words had chilled me, frightened me. I ran after her and grasped her arm. "I am telling you the truth. He is very ill. Aunt Charlotte!" I cried. "There is no need for her to verify what I have said. All this time we are wasting may mean life or death for Grandfather!"

I could see the uncertainty on Aunt Charlotte's face, as though she feared to press the other woman too far. Then quickly, with a last authoritative gesture, she said, "Yes, we must waste no time. You had better get Julio and have him go and fetch a doctor."

Cieta gave her a considering look and finally shrugged. "It shall be as you say." Then her voice sharpened. "But as soon as he is well, they will have to go. You understand that, Lottie? You will have to send them away. Julio is in the garden. You can go and call him."

For a moment neither woman moved. I

sensed something between them, a battle of wills. I could not understand its reason and was concerned only with my own worry.

"Will you please hurry?" I shouted out. "By the time the doctor gets here, it may be too late!"

The stiffness went out of Aunt Charlotte's body. She hurried out through the kitchen door. I heard her voice calling and a few moments later a man came trailing in behind her. At my first glance at him, I decided that he was Cieta's husband. They were both dark-skinned, although he was much more so than she, both had the same high-cheeked case of features and spoke with the same singsong cadence in their voices. He said, "You have want of me—yes?"

But Julio was much the older of the two, almost middle-aged in fact. He had a face ruined by pock marks, a thin body already beginning to shrink, and black, greasy hair, a lock of which hung down over his forehead. The two were ill-matched, she with her great beauty and air of authority and he who did not raise his eyes when she spoke to him. She would never have married this craven creature.

He was evidently the man-of-all-work around Balcktower. I saw that his hands were soil-grimed and I could detect the odor of horses and stables about him.

Cieta gave him his orders as though he were something less than human, a pack animal, a work horse who could only understand the voice tone and not the words of a harsh command. There was careless contempt in her manner when she repeated the instructions again as she might have to a dim-witted child.

When she had finished, the ugly little man looked up and I saw his eyes, as black and shiny as her own, and what I saw in them made me shiver. It was a flash of pure hatred. It was a glare so bright that I expected her to shrivel under it.

But she merely laughed aloud and said, "Go, Julio! Whip the horse and get back as soon as you can. You are not to linger in the village. And talk to no one. Merely tell the doctor to come. If he asks you questions you are not to answer them."

He slunk away with shuffling feet and with his head drooping again. Cieta turned to me and said, "You had better get upstairs. It will be, perhaps, an hour before the doctor gets back. Surely there is something you can do for the old man in the meantime."

So I went back to Grandfather. I waited in his room, listening to his labored breathing, coaxing water into the parched old lips, holding his hand for no reason except that I was frightened and felt impelled to cling to him.

It seemed like many hours, rather than one, that I waited, but finally footsteps sounded in the hall and the door opened. Cieta came into the room and behind her was a tall man in a dark ulster who carried a small black bag in his hand.

For an instant we stared at each other, the doctor and I. Then he said in that deep voice I had heard before when he had asked me if I needed help, "I am Dr. Andrew Bruce."

Only that. This man, who had seemed familiar to me because I had dreamed my girlish dreams about someone like him, looked at me as coldly and impersonally as though we had never set eyes upon each other before. There was no smile, no spark of recognition in his eyes. His face looked chiseled and remote. And he turned away from me after that brief moment and followed Cieta to the bedside.

She remained there while he examined Grandfather. When he spoke it was only to her. I stood at the other side of the bed and my eyes kept lifting to look at Dr. Bruce. There was something that drew my glance as though by a magnet, yet he seemed to be unaware of my presence.

His attention was concentrated on his patient. And then Cieta spoke to him and he turned his head to her. I saw his face change, the look of interest that brightened his eyes. They roamed her features carefully. Her lilting voice seemed to be weaving some sort of magic spell about him for he was as unmoving as though he were hypnotized.

I stood watching them and it seemed that they had moved out of the world I inhabited and were in a different one. A feeling of heaviness began to spread inside me and I had to turn away.

CHAPTER THREE

I did not have to look at Andrew Bruce's face to see it. Those strong, well-defined features were beginning to etch themselves into my mind. He was clean-shaven and thus different from any doctor I had ever known; I had believed that a beard was the badge of a physician. Yet his lack of one did nothing to diminish his dignity in spite of his youth. He could not have been more than twenty-seven or -eight; his skin was firm and faintly browned from the outdoors; there was the briskness of vigor about his movements.

Because I could not keep my gaze averted too long, I glanced at him again and found his eyes upon me. They held a considering, thoughtful look and I knew that he had not forgotten that brief meeting in front of the livery stable. Then Cieta spoke to him again, asked him some inconsequential question, and I lost his attention.

How could I have retained it in the face of her vibrant beauty? I saw her smile at him, watched the play of a dimple cut into her cheek, the sweep of her incredibly long, silky eyelashes. And I felt myself shrink into color-lessness, I whose only attractions were my "good" skin and hair and quiet gray eyes which were perhaps too grave for a girl of twenty.

She said on a lingering and reluctant note, "I must leave you for a few moments. There is something I must do," and she went from the room with a swinging, graceful step.

He watched her until she was out of sight and only then turned to me, spoke to me directly for the first time since his arrival. "Tell me more about the patient. Who was with him during the night? Was it you?"

"He was sleeping. At least I believed he was. This morning I found him——found him like this."

"You did not take his temperature?"

"I do not know if there is a thermometer in the house and I did not think to bring one with us. Doctor, is he seriously ill?" My voice sounded thin and distracted and not at all, of course, as attractive as Cieta's. "He will not——will not die, will he?"

"I think not, Miss——Miss Lawson, is it? But he is in poor condition. A heart as old as this one becomes badly strained by a long journey. You came from Boston, didn't you? There was that and there seems to be a little congestion in the lungs."

I wondered how he had learned my name and where we had come from, and then I decided that Cieta must have told him certain things while she was showing him upstairs. What else had she told him, what reason had she given him for our being there? I did not feel that I could ask him those questions.

He asked me about Grandfather's medical history and, as briefly as I could, I recounted it. And then he said that the patient must be kept quiet, that there must be no excitement, most important of all no emotional upsets.

"But I had hoped——"

I bit back what I had been about to say. I had almost blurted out that I intended to take Grandfather away immediately. It would mean explaining my eagerness to get away and the reasons for it and I could not reveal anything like that to him. He was a virtual stranger in spite of my strange feeling of having known him for a long time.

"Yes, Miss Lawson?"

He was waiting for me to speak and I blushed like a confused schoolgirl. Andrew Bruce seemed to have the power to drag up from within me an emotion I had never known before. My heart began to beat more rapidly under the gaze of those dark-brown eyes and I found the sensation disturbing.

I had always prided myself on my self-discipline and good sense. When I had gone to live with Grandfather eight years before, after the deaths of my parents, we had both expected that he would be taking care of me. It had proved to be the other way around, however, and tending an aging man, whose health was even then failing, had made me responsible and level-headed beyond my years. Yet here I stood tongue-tied and flushed while this stranger studied me with his probing glance. And then the spell of his eyes was broken because Cieta came back into the room and his head swiveled immediately in her direction.

She asked, "Are you ready to leave, Doctor? I will show you to the door."

He put on his coat and started after her, and then before he reached the door he came back, moved around the bed so that he was standing beside me and spoke in a low voice. "If you need me at any time, do not hesitate to send for me. And Miss Lawson, as soon as he is able to leave, go back to where you came from." He craned his neck to make sure that Cieta was not within earshot and then added, "I mean it! Get out of here the first moment you can!"

I was too astonished to speak. His urgent words seemed to echo in the room and then Cieta called out, "Doctor? Are you ready?"

He whispered to me, "Do not forget what I said. And remember to give him the pills every four hours without fail. Do that your-self; let no one else take care of him."

And then he was gone; I heard him speak to Cieta and their footsteps grew fainter as they went down the hall. I stood there wondering if I had imagined it all. For why would Doctor Bruce feel impelled to urge me to leave the house? His words had been a warning, there was no doubt about that. But what was he cautioning me against? What did he know about this strange, frightening house and the people in it?

The following day he came again to see Grandfather and I longed to ask him then. We were alone. I had no idea where Cieta was, for I had not left the room all day. And it was Julio who brought up on a tray my breakfast and luncheon and a bowl of gruel for Grandfather.

With just the two of us there, and Grandfather who was too close to unconsciousness to hear what we were saying, I longed to ask Doctor Bruce what his words had meant. And to tell him what the hack driver had said about "quareness" in the house and to recount the strange happenings of the night before last.

But I was held back by the doctor's cool manner. He seemed withdrawn and remote; evidently he was a man of rapidly-changing moods, for he showed no concern for me or interest in me. He spoke in a professional way about his patient, explained to me about the dangers of heart failure, so tersely that I felt chilled. I might have been one of his nurses taking his orders. So I cloaked my hurt pride and disappointment in a manner as aloof as his own. He must be feeling, I thought, something like my own disappointment. For it had been

Julio who had accompanied him upstairs this time and there could have been no hoped-for meeting with Cieta.

Then, once more, he said something which shocked me with surprise. He had gone to the washstand in the corner and was pouring water over his hands. Not looking at me and speaking almost casually, he said, "It must be hard with two patients in the house. But I suppose Mrs. Prescott and the girl take care of the other one?"

I repeated foolishly, "Two? The other one?"

"The young man. Isn't there a young man who is chronically ill and remains in his bed all the time?"

My head began to shake back and forth mechanically. He turned and looked at me, and although his words had been off-hand, now there was a sharp light in his eyes. He stood there with the towel in his hand, not using it but letting it dangle from his fingers.

"I don't know what you're talking about," I said faintly. "I know of no one else sick in this house."

"Alicia! Listen to me, you must do as I told you yesterday. This is no place for you and I don't want you to linger here longer than necessary. It is dangerous."

His use of my first name and the sudden change in his tone confused me. It was a moment or two before I could ask, "Why? Dr. Bruce, you must tell me. You say these things, do not explain them and leave me to puzzle and wonder."

"I can tell you nothing more. Not now."

He picked up his bag, threw his coat over his arm and strode from the room. But even when he was gone his presence seemed to linger and I could not get him out of my mind.

During the days that followed, I thought of him often, let myself daydream about him. It was a way of lightening the monotony of my sickroom vigils while the hours stretched, long and dreary, until I almost lost track of time.

It was a way, too, of keeping at bay the terror that seemed to live with me all those days and nights. When darkness came, I would feel apprehension stealing over me again. I would listen for footsteps in the hall; awake with a start from drowsing, imagining that I was about to be pounced upon from some shadowy corner. When I had to go to my room from Grandfather's and then back again down that short stretch of hall, my nerves tingled and I would feel my heart begin to pound. I sensed that the house held always the threat of danger, remembering too well the night when someone had tried to kill me, the ominous words of the hack driver, Dr. Bruce's warning.

And yet nothing happened. The house remained wrapped in stillness at night; no one came to our rooms except Julio and, occasionally, Cieta. They brought trays of food to me and fresh linen for the beds and took away the soiled sheets and Grandfather's night shirts and my own clothing and brought them back laundered.

They spoke to me only when there was something necessary to be said. Cieta's eyes never met mine but I would feel her gaze on me and my skin would sting and prickle until she left the room. I was afraid of her, and I longed for the day when Grandfather and I would be able to leave Blacktower.

I gave routine care—adminstering the pills, bathing the thin old body, changing the bed-clothing. Grandfather would awaken now and then, smile at me dimly, stretch out his frail hand to be held. He would murmur my name, although he did not seem to know where he was, only that I was there to take care of him.

His face, once rosy and round like Aunt Charlotte's, had shrunk and its soft, creased skin hung in loose folds. His sweeping moustache and his hair, long and silvery, had grown dry and brittle. There were times when the waiting for him to grow better seemed unendurable and I longed to send for Doctor Bruce. But I could not be sure of my true motives, whether I was actually apprehensive about Grandfather or looking for an excuse to see Andrew again. I thought of him now as "Andrew" and I hoped that he would come of his own accord, but he did not and I did

44

not send for him, and so there was no one to reassure me or share the burden of my fear and worry.

More and more I looked forward to the day when I would be free.

"Free." It was a strange word and yet I recognized its implications. There was no reason at any time for me to leave our two rooms and I did not. I was certain that Cieta or Aunt Charlotte——perhaps both in common agreement——had arranged things thus in an effort to keep me from wandering around the house. What secret was it hiding that I must be kept a virtual prisoner? I had the desolate feeling of being completely cut off from the world.

A "nightmare," Cieta had said in explanation of the attempt that had been made on my life. But I knew differently, although now everything had a nightmarish quality about it. I felt that if I did not soon get away from Blacktower I was in danger of losing my mind.

I watched Grandfather's progress anxiously. I prepared in my mind the arguments I would use to persuade him to let me take him back to Boston when he was well enough to travel. I tried to think of words which would let him know how frightening and repellent Blacktower had become to me without unduly alarming him, because Andrew Bruce had stressed the need to keep his patient free of emotional upset. But somehow I must make him see that our coming here had been a grave mistake.

Finally he began to grow stronger, sitting up for a little while each day and taking the spoonfuls of gruels and soups I fed him. One day I even managed to get him out of bed and on his feet, and although he was weak and dizzied by the effort, I was cheered by the little accomplishment.

From then on I kept him propped higher on his pillows and made him stand and walk for short periods of time. His color began to return and his breathing was almost normal again.

There came a morning when he no longer needed constant attention and I could not resist the temptation to leave our small quarters for a little while. The decision did not come easily nor hastily, for the passing days had not dulled the memory of that shadowy figure which had crept into my room on the first night of our arrival. But it was broad daylight and I sensed somehow that Aunt Charlotte would not allow harm to come to her brother. I allowed myself to be reassured by remembering how she had pitted her will against Cieta's in the matter of having a doctor for him.

While he was sleeping, I threw my cloak around me and hurried out into the hall, planning to leave him for only a little while. Through the window which I passed I could see that the weather had turned warm and spring-like. The sky was a cloudless blue and the sunlight was bright and golden. Surely nothing evil could happen on such a beautiful day!

And yet I moved quietly as I went down to the first floor. I prayed that I would meet no one, for I did not want it known that I had left Grandfather alone. And I was sure that those who had kept me a virtual prisoner on the second floor for so long would not look with favor on my wandering around the grounds.

Near the entrance, on the opposite side from the bulging tower wall, a door stood open. I went through it and found myself on a terrace which ran along the side of the house. It was partly enclosed by a shoulder-high balustrade and at the end of the terrace were steps leading down to a narrow path.

To my right, lawns of withered brown grass fell in a slight slope and then became overgrown with low shrubbery which thickened into woodlands. On my left, beyond the terrace, was a herb garden flanked by stables and outbuildings.

The path led past them and I followed it, curious as to where it would take me. There was a hushed stillness around me with only the soft padding of my footsteps falling into it. The sun beat down on my face with a lovely warmth. I could feel my feet growing springier, a sense of release lightening my spirits, and I hated the thought that this short interlude of freedom must soon end and that I would have to return to the gloom of Captain Lawson's castle with its ever-present atmosphere of lurking danger.

When I was about to turn, I looked ahead and saw a rising slope a little way beyond the outbuildings. Small white objects glistened in the sunlight and I went forward curiously to see what they were. I came upon a clearing and then a cemetery. The little white objects were gravestones.

It seemed like a strange place to find a burial ground, although I must have been aware that many large estates, especially those in isolated areas, had their own small cemeteries. I felt impelled to go closer and examine the markers. This must be, after all, the final resting place of some of my ancestors. No doubt the man who had built Blacktower would be buried here.

I had no trouble finding his grave. Above it was a huge stone with the outlines of a compass and a telescope engraved upon it. The epitaph—and I guessed immediately that Aunt Charlotte had composed it—was: "CAPT. SIMEON LAWSON, AT REST CLOSE TO THE SEA HE LOVED AFTER A LONG LIFE OF SERVICE TO HIS GOD AND FELLOW-MAN. BORN SEPT. 19, 1808. DIED JAN. 6, 1885."

Beside him, under a smaller stone, was his wife. "HANNAH BARNES LAWSON," the inscription read. She had been born in 1803 and had died at the untimely age of thirty-five.

Close to the graves of their parents were those of three little children who had died in infancy, the two brothers and a sister of Grandfather and Aunt Charlotte. I wandered about and found the burial plot of Thomas Prescott, the captain's son-in-law, and those of servants who had died while serving at Blacktower.

But I passed, too, plots which were unmarked, although it was plain from their shapes that there were coffins beneath them. I found that fact puzzling, for there were a dozen or more of such graves without stones or any other way of determining who was buried in them. Some looked fairly new. On one or two the sod had sunk and there was a tangle of weeds growing over them.

I could spend no more time there, at any rate. I knew that I had wandered too far and stayed over-long. I turned and started back toward the house and in my haste I did not look carefully enough where I was going. And so I stumbled over a mound of dirt and, if I had not regained my balance quickly enough, I would have fallen into the deep hole which yawned at my feet.

I had almost tumbled into an empty grave. There was no doubt about what it was, that pit which gaped somehow obscenely in a remote part of the cemetery. It was wide enough and long enough to hold a coffin. The depth of the hole, which I looked down into with fascinated horror, must be the traditional six feet used for burial purposes.

In that moment of utter stillness, I heard the soft, murmuring cooing of a pigeon on the stable roof. The sound was like a mournful dirge and I turned in the direction instinctively. But it was not only the bird's voice which drew my glance to the outbuildings and then to the big house itself. An uneasy chill was spreading over my nerves. I sensed that some-one was watching me.

It was a terrifying thing to stand there alone in that open space and know that hidden eyes were upon me. I thought of Julio who, I guessed, had his living quarters in the barn or one of the other small buildings. But I saw no sign of the dark, pockmarked little man nor of anyone else.

I hurried down the path that ran through the row of graves, and now there was no magic in the sun-drenched day, no comforting warmth to touch my face and make it glow. I could see no promise of spring in the bar-renness around me.

As I ran toward the lane which led to the stone terrace, my body tingled and shivered, and I was panting and gasping. So I stopped for a moment, for I did not want anyone I might meet in the house to see me looking like a wild, frightened thing.

In that moment I felt again, even more certainly this time, that someone was watching me. I lifted my head and my eyes were drawn upward, almost against my will it seemed, to the flat surface of the house in front of me. This was a sheer, blank wall with none of the jutting ornamentation that spread itself above and beside the front entrance. Only the rows of windows were cut into the brick. And so I could see far up to the top story with the battlemented roof rising above it.

I could not have helped myself from lifting my gaze in that direction. It was almost as though my gaze were being magnetized.

High in one of the narrow windows, in what must have been the fourth story, I saw something small and round flash in the sunlight. It looked like an oversized eyeglass lens and I guessed immediately what it was.

Perhaps I recognized it because I had seen, only a few minutes ago, the carving of a spyglass on Captain Lawson's tombstone. My face and body magnified by the telescope, I would have been observed plainly, while wandering around the cemetery, by the one who stood there looking through it.

The flash of light disappeared. And then as I stood there unable to wrench my eyes away, I glimpsed a face made narrow by the sides of the window. It disappeared almost immediately and I stood rooted in the shadow of the huge, ugly house, the monstrous place which waited for my return.

There was no sound, no movement. The blank pane of glass stared back at me and even the mourning pigeon was silent.

CHAPTER FOUR

Who had been there at the top-story window? I thought of Cieta and Aunt Charlotte but, in my brief glimpse of the face, it had seemed that its lines were masculine. Julio? But the skin had looked too pale for his, even blurred as it had been by glass and distance.

Nor could I guess how long someone had been observing me——I'd had only that vague feeling of being watched——nor whether I'd been seen when I stumbled over the mound of dirt beside the empty grave. The implication of that gaping hole had sped my feet on my way back to the house, but now they felt weighted and leaden, and my footsteps echoed loudly on the stone floor of the terrace. The side door was still open and I went through it as quietly as I could.

Again I met no one, heard no sounds of voices nor of any activity anywhere. I could not imagine how the others who lived in the house spent all the hours of their days. It was evident that there was no communication of any sort with the outside world. Except for the morning when Julio went to fetch the doctor, I had never heard the clopping of horses' hoofs nor the clattering of the farm wagon on the road leading from the house.

It occurred to me that the manservant and Cieta and Aunt Charlotte must live a sort of prison-like existence of their own and I wondered why my grandfather's sister had allowed herself to be confined here at Blacktower in such a dismal form of living. But perhaps she had become so used to the routine of enthrallment that she was still bound by the habit of it. Yet Simeon Lawson had been dead for fifteen years. She would have been in her early fifties at the time of his death——young enough, surely, to have begun a new life for herself.

Grandfather had spoken of Captain Lawson's great wealth, the fortune he had amassed in his sailing days. Unless she were an actual miser, Aunt Charlotte could have spent her inherited money in traveling or social activities.

It occurred to me then that herein might lie the answer to my grandaunt's hostile and frightened attitude. Perhaps she feared that her brother had come to lay claim to his share of the money.

Hostile and frightened. It did not quite describe the way she had looked the night she came downstairs and found us there. Not so much greed had been on her face as cringing horror.

There was no one I could talk to about these things. Not Grandfather, surely, for although he seemed well enough when I went up to his room that day after my walk, he was still weak and unable to sustain interest for very long in anything that was said to him. And while he seemed to grow stronger in the days that followed, I came to realize that something was happening to his mind.

The first time this knowledge pressed upon me was one morning when I took him for a short walk as far as the hall window. There was nothing to see except the ocean, no ships anywhere in sight. This was a treacherous stretch of shore with its massed formation of rocks as far as one could see in either direction and others, undoubtedly, hidden by the waves.

Grandfather stood looking out silently for a while and then he said in a petulant, boyish voice, "Father promised to take me with him on his next voyage. He has gone without me."

My heart grew cold as I looked at him and finally he turned to look at me. "Father was angry with me. Perhaps that is why he didn't take me."

His eyes, so faded that almost all color was washed from them, were as vacant as a child's. I could not draw a full breath; pain, heavy and dull, was spreading throughout my insides. He was all I had had since the death of my parents. And I loved him with a protective fierceness. I could not bear that mindless glaze of his eyes, the pettish notes in the cracked old voice.

Since our arrival at Blacktower, he had absorbed all my time and most of my thoughts. I was still afraid for myself; my sleep was broken by the restlessness of fear and malaise, but he was much more helpless than I. No longer was I sure that Aunt Charlotte would protect him, for she never set foot in his room.

When I had seen that empty grave in the cemetery, thoughts of Grandfather had sprung immediately into my mind. I had not thought of myself then, but now I knew that the gaping hole could be waiting for either one of us. Or, possibly, both.

Always there was this sense of impending peril and now this——Grandfather's mind captured by the long-ago past——shocked me. I did not know, at that moment, what had actually happened to him but I sensed that we would be safer back in his room. Even in the daylight hours this shadowy corridor seemed to represent danger. And below the window were the sharp and craggy rocks of the ledge, and beyond them was the muttering sea. And from out there I had heard the tolling of a bell, coming from whence I did not know. This was one of the secrets of Blacktower and even the thought of it pulled my nerves into tautness.

By the time I got Grandfather into bed he was babbling almost incoherently. "He does not understand that I do not want to follow in his footsteps. . . . I would like to go on a voyage or two, but not make it my life as it is his. . . . He is angry and seeks to punish me in many different ways. . . ."

I was almost frantic as I sat there and listened to him. Never had I felt so utterly helpless. He fell asleep still talking.

During the days that followed, he scarcely ever came out of the distant world he had slipped into. He spoke of things that had happened fifty-five years ago as though he were experiencing them at that moment. He talked of Charlotte, the young Lottie; of their mother and father; of a dog named Horatio and a parrot named Christopher Columbus. He talked as though they were all still alive.

It was a period of heartache for me. I was torn between pity and worry. If I could only get him to Boston, I knew, there would be help for him in one of the hospitals there. Only recently I had read articles in the *Boston Globe* and *Harper's Weekly* about the new methods being used by doctors these days in the care of people with troubled minds.

As gently as I could I broached the subject of going home. He was sitting up in a chair that day, his withered hands clasped over the blanket that covered his legs, a dreamy look in his eyes.

"Grandfather," I said, stroking his hair lightly, "you are not happy here, are you?"

It took a little while for the question to penetrate his clouded brain. Then he said, "I would be happy if I were not so disobedient and lacking in filial love. Father has shown me the way to be happy, by following his orders, but I have been rebellious and stubborn. No matter, I shall tell him I'm sorry and that I'll do what he asks of me."

I knew nothing about the new science called "psychiatry" with which an Austrian doctor was making quite a stir; but I realized what had happened to Grandfather. In an effort to erase a boyhood guilt, he had traveled back more than half-a-century and lost himself in a happy fantasy. In it he was the kind of son his father had wanted him to be. I must make him come back from that dream where he was young once more and always approved of and loved.

"Grandfather, we cannot stay here!" My voice rose in urgency. "We must go home to Boston. You are well enough to travel now. There is a man here who will drive us to the village and we could take the train——"

I broke off because I saw that he was becoming agitated. His head jerked upward and his hands flew into the air as though invisible strings were moving them.

"No! No! I will not go away! This is my home. I must stay here and wait for Father to come back and take me on his next journey. I do not want to go to Boston! It is dirty there. The streets run with filth. It is a long ride on the coach and people traveling meet all sort of lawbreakers——thieves, robbers, bandits!"

I quieted him as best I could, knowing only too well that an emotional outburst of this sort was bad for his health. Dr. Bruce had cautioned me to keep him calm and happy and I feared the effect this little scene had had upon him.

Later, I promised myself, I would try again. For I hoped that this was only a temporary thing, a passing aberration. With time he might come back into the real world and then I would be able to make definite plans for our departure. So I told myself. I could not face the prospect of remaining at Blacktower much longer. My spirits were depressed from remaining in the two small, ill-furnished rooms and the hours seemed to drag endlessly. One could not live with fear indefinitely and sometimes I became lethargic and even wished that something would happen to bring out into the open whatever it was that I felt was threatening us.

I kept thinking back to the puzzles of the house—the clanging bell, the voices behind the tower wall, why someone had wanted me dead, the face at the fourth-floor window. That last began to possess my mind more and more. Who was it who had looked out at me? I knew nothing about the house except that it was big and dark and chilly and filled with some strange, ominous atmosphere. It was time I learned more about it and so one mid-morning I summoned my courage and decided to investigate this one mystery at least.

Nothing, I told myself, could happen to me at this time of day. No one would be coming to our rooms until noon, as our breakfast trays had been brought to us by Julio and then taken away with the used bedlinen. Grandfather had fallen back to sleep and I was free again for a little while.

As I went down the hall I paused long enough to look out the side window. From there I could see the herb garden and in it two figures, Cieta's and Aunt Charlotte's, were bent over a patch of earth. Seeing them digging there crystallized my purpose. I knew I would never have a better opportunity for what I intended to do.

At the staircase landing I stopped and looked up. The steps wound upward to dizzying heights, all curves and bends. There were no sounds from anywhere, only thick oppressive silence, and I could feel the trembling of my hand as it slid along the banister. I was afraid to look back and down and it seemed as though I would never reach the top.

I came to the third floor. Nothing here, either, except half-gloom and the long, dark hall with doors shut on either side of it and the bulge of the tower wall at my left, that rounded protuberance that seemed to dominate the house with its ugliness. I could hear my own breathing, sharp and ragged, as I climbed the last flight of stairs.

Here on the fourth floor the ceiling was lower and so the shadows were thicker, the hall even darker. There seemed to be fewer rooms on this story where the structure of the house narrowed. And here, too, all the doors along the hall were closed. I tried to guess which room contained the window at which I had seen a face.

It would be on the north side, to my right as I walked away from the staircase, and I tried the first doorknob I came to and found it unlatched.

I drew a deep breath, hesitated there for a moment to quiet the fluttering inside me. I didn't know what I would find on the other side of the door. I realized now that I had let myself be drawn up here by a foolhardy purpose. I might be walking into physical danger. Yet it was too late now to turn back. Having come this far, I had to go on. Cautiously and quietly I twisted the knob, pushed open the door and went a few steps over the threshold.

The first thing I noticed, when I tiptoed into the room, was the strange, sweetish odor that hung in the air. It was not exactly unpleasant but, rather, strong and pungent. It was not unlike the smell of a sickroom but heavier, more pervasive.

Until my eyes became used to the gloom, I could see little. Then the outlines of the furnishings began to emerge. A fireplace ran along one wall; heavy pieces of furniture crowded each other; there was a clutter of smaller pieces. The bed had a huge, carved headboard which stretched almost to the ceiling. The man who lay among the pillows under it looked almost lost.

I stood staring at him, mouth agape, for what seemed a long time. At first he did not know I was there, for his eyes were closed, but then he opened them, as though brought out of sleep by my gaze and I said hastily, "I hope I haven't frightened you. If I'm intruding just tell me and I'll go away."

He did not seem frightened or anything else at all. There was no emotion in his face. It was blank, as a person's face becomes blank in sleep, and I thought that perhaps he was not yet quite aware of me.

I have described him as a man, but actually he appeared to be scarcely more than a youth. I guessed that he was not more than a year or two older than I for there was a look of boyishness about all that I could see of him—pale tousled hair and delicate skin as fine and smooth as a baby's. He was pale and his eyes, the color of sea water on a warm day, looked enormous in his face.

"If you are ill," I said, backing away, "you probably don't want me here. I'd better go."

"No, no, stay!" He took a hand from beneath the bedclothes to gesture toward a chair and I saw how white it was, how prominently the blue viens on it stood out.

Before I could sit down, I had to clear from a chair the books and magazines and newspapers that were piled on it. The untidy appearance of the room was due, I suppose, to his being confined to bed. Most of the clutter was caused by the things he used to amuse himself with——novels and adventure stories, notebooks and pencils, a set of paints. A gramophone with a horn like a giant morning glory stood on a table in one corner of the room. Around the bed were scattered papers which I recognized as marine charts. I felt a pang in my heart for this handsome, personable boy who undoubtedly loved the sea but who saw it only from his fourth-floor window.

As my eyes returned to him, I took note of the objects on the bedside table, a telescope and a pair of field glasses. I knew now who had spied upon me, but I felt no anger at the discovery. By the collection of things in the room I could guess that he had been confined here for a long time. If it amused him, or lightened the long, monotonous hours for him, I could not begrudge him his little diversion.

I smiled warmly at him, feeling suddenly lighthearted and relieved for the first time in days. Now one mystery at least was solved. Perhaps when I came to know this boy better he would tell me the answers to the others.

There was that and there was the fact that I was starved for companionship with someone my own age. He did not appear to be actually ill; nor were there any signs about him of the fear that plagued me continually. He returned my smile and seemed to be waiting for me to speak.

I said, "I haven't told you my name. I'm Alicia Lawson. My grandfather and I came for a visit. Did you know that?"

He nodded. "Yes, I knew. I suppose I should call you 'Alicia,' since we must be about the same age. And why don't you call me 'Craig'?"

I waited but he did not reveal the rest of his name. We studied each other for a moment or two longer. And in that time I decided that he was by far the most attractive man I had ever seen. His eyes were deep blue and now they were no longer dull and placid; something glittered in them, perhaps it was excitement. No doubt he had few visitors here in this remote house cut off from the world. I was glad now that I had come.

I picked a book at random from the bedside table and asked him if he had enjoyed reading it. He returned that he did not like Thackeray, that he found him stilted and pretentious. I argued the point hotly for I had liked every single page of *Vanity Fair* and Thackeray was one of my favorite authors.

When I realized what was happening, that a boy I had seen for the first time only a few moments ago was engaged with me in a near-quarrel, I broke off. But he merely laughed when I apologized. His laughter was a lovely sound (I realized that I had not heard any for a long time) although rather high-pitched and shrill.

We went on discussing, though with more restraint now, our favorite authors and books and composers and music. I found that he had amazing knowledge of all sorts of things for someone who evidently never went beyond the walls of his room. I meant to ask him about that, inquire as to the nature of his illness, when we grew to know each other better.

Right then it was merely pleasant to sit and talk with someone my own age; I did not want to spoil it with prying questions. And I relinquished, too, my intention to tell him about the fear that pressed upon me every waking hour, my worry about Grandfather, my apprehension that something would happen to one of us or both before I could get us away. He was talking rapidly, his eyes bright and eager, and he was much more lively than he had been when our conversation started. I felt that the little interlude was doing him good and I did not want to spoil it for him.

But there ran under my thoughts puzzlement over why I had not been aware of his presence here in the house before. Yet who would tell me? I seldom laid eyes on Aunt Charlotte. I was scarcely on speaking terms with Julio and my fear of Cieta kept me tongued-tied when she was about. If it had not been for Andrew

Bruce, I should not have known that Craig existed.

"I keep calling you 'Craig,'" I said, "but I do not even know your last name. Is it a secret?"

"Of course not!" His voice sharpened. "It is 'Prescott'. Now is there anything else you want to know?"

I was afraid that I had offended him, for he sounded testy although I could not understand why he would take umbrage at my question.

Prescott. Since he bore the same name as Aunt Charlotte, he must be a relative of her husband; had been, that is, since Thomas Prescott was dead. Why, then, hadn't Grandfather mentioned that the boy was living here if, indeed, he knew?

I had no opportunity to ask any more questions because Craig embarked on a series of his own. Why had I come to Blacktower? How long did we intend to stay? Was it true that my grandfather had collapsed on the night of his arrival and was still in poor health?

Someone, evidently, had been telling him things about us. Whoever it was——Cieta or Julio or Aunt Charlotte——who cared for him. Perhaps he had heard the coming of the doctor or my voice and had inquired.

And then suddenly, while I was still answering him, his interest began to flag. His attention seemed to wander and he grew restless.

His eyes made little sorties in all directions and his hands clenched and unclenched on the bedclothes.

"You had better go!" he burst out abruptly. "It is not right for you to be here."

My voice broke off in mid-sentence. I felt dashed. Only a moment ago he had seemed to like having me with him. He had been talking brightly, smiled at me, even laughed aloud. Now he was dismissing me in a harsh voice and there was hostility in his stare.

I wondered if perhaps there had flowed over him an awareness of the difference between us. I was healthy, strong; while his little world was bound by the bed he lay in and, perhaps, the window where he could see the other world only through his telescope or field glasses. Perhaps, deep down in his heart, he resented me. He might be a moody invalid who enjoyed the small power of being able to order someone from his room if he desired.

Yet I could not actually believe that. There had been something appealing about him when I first came——a sweetness of nature, amiability. The change in him was even more bewildering because of that.

I was neither angry nor hurt. What filled my heart was pity for him. I said gently, "Of course I will go if you want me to, Craig. But I'll come back some time when you're feeling better. Perhaps you'd like to play a game or have me read to you. Do you like Authors or checkers? I'm very good at checkers. I play with Grandfather often. Do you have a checkerboard?"

He did not answer me either with words or a motion of his head. He merely stared at me with eyes that glittered more brightly than ever, and I could see the faint shine of perspiration that lay at his hairline. I decided that he must be feeling the first enthrallment of pain and did not want me to see him in its throes.

And so I got up hastily and pushed back my chair. "Goodbye, Craig. I will come again soon now that Grandfather does not need me every moment."

I had discovered only a little of what I had come to learn. I had not sought for and thus not received explanations of anything except who had been spying on me when I was in the graveyard. Later, I promised myself. The next time I came I would lead gradually up to the questions I wanted to ask.

I was thinking of how I could best put those questions as I was on my way to the door. Then, before I reached it, I heard soft footsteps coming along the hall. I drew back instinctively; somehow I knew that the others in the house would not want me visiting this boy. They had been careful to arrange things so that I would not have reason to leave Grandfather's room and my own. And there was something that hinted of secrecy in Craig's being up here on the fourth floor when there must be so many vacant rooms in Blacktower.

The footsteps slowed down and then sounded on the threshold. I was standing there like a guilty child caught in mischief when I looked into the face of Cieta.

She held in her hands a tray with a glass and bottles on it. There had been a faint smile on her face, but it died quickly at the sight of me. Her chiseled features hardened and her eyes grew brighter and even darker.

For an instant we stared at each other, our gazes locked. Then she pushed past me and went to Craig's bedside. Her glance roamed over him and now her face had begun to melt and become softened. I had never seen her wear this expression before. I would have guessed that there was no tenderness in her, for she was one of the things that frightened me most about Blacktower.

The gentle moment passed. She swung back in my direction. Her black eyes raked over me. I could almost feel their sharpness on my skin. No one had ever looked at me in that way before, pouring out over me a savage and murderous hatred. It all showed without restraint ——unconcealed jealousy and fury that she had found us there alone together.

I knew that she would have gladly killed me at that moment.

CHAPTER FIVE

There was something fiercely possessive about the way she stood beside Craig's bed, her body blocking my view of his face. I shrank away and turned but even when I was on my way to the door, I could feel her bitter gaze on my back.

That night I heard noises again. For a long time I had lain sleepless, worrying about my grandfather and more sharply afraid for my own safety because I had incurred Cieta's open enmity. I knew that there would be no further delay; I must get us away from Black-tower quickly.

When sleep finally came, it was deep and dreamless. I came partly awake at the darkest hour of the night and I had to struggle up through layers of drowsiness and lethargy.

The noises sounded far away at first, for my ears were not yet alert. The clanging of the bell was faint yet unmistakable. Then, some time later, came the murmuring of muffled voices and the shuffling of footsteps on the rocks.

If there was moaning and weeping in the tower that night I did not hear it, for my door was tightly shut with a chair placed in front of it, as there had been since someone had invaded my room. I could not have gone even as far as the door to listen; a great weight of fear seemed to be pressing down on me and the sense of evil and danger pervaded my room until it was almost like some ugly, tangible thing. There was no more sleep for me that night, only a restless tossing and listening.

In the morning I went to the hall window and looked out. And again I saw nothing. The sunlight on the water had a crystal quality, sharp and glittering. The sight of it gave me no pleasure. More fearful than ever, I was trying to figure out a way to get out of Blacktower. I knew that I would have to enlist the help of someone.

I had no one to turn to except Aunt Charlotte. When I had dressed, I went in search of her.

On my way downstairs, I thought of the things I would say to her. I decided to appeal to her family loyalty. Surely some remnant of feeling must remain for her brother. Whatever else there might be in her life now——Cieta's influence or some secret they shared——Grandfather had been her father's son. There was that. And old common memories should have formed some sort of bond between them.

I found her in a first-floor room which had evidently been Captain Lawson's study. It held huge old chairs and a roll-top desk. There was a ship's binnacle in one corner, its brass surface burnished to a mirror-like

71

gloss. A wooden figurehead stood upon a marble stand. A number of ship models, one in a green glass bottle, crowded the tops of the cabinets that lined the walls.

Aunt Charlotte was on her knees in front of one of the cabinets. Its door was open and she held a piece of soft cloth in one of her hands and a small silver object in the other. The shelves were full of other things, statuettes and figurines of jade and ivory and teakwood.

She was still the vestal virgin, I thought. Still tending the votive fires to her personal god in this housewifely way. I looked about curiously. There were a great many strange and exotic small articles, most of them locked behind glass doors, all of them undoubtedly of great value and collected by Captain Lawson during his sea-going days.

Many, many things——I could not have counted them all. Joss idols of ebony and ivory Buddhas, silver temple bells, jade necklaces, fierce-looking knives and a collection of articles made of scrimshaw, those last the sort of things fashioned of whalebone by sailors during long, time-dragging journeys.

Aunt Charlotte got up from her knees slowly. Her round little face was pale this morning. It was cold and unsmiling as she looked across the room at me. But then this seemed to be her habitual expression. I had never seen her smile, not once in the few times I had come upon her by chance. But her eyes showed something besides hostility this morning— pain, I thought—as we gazed at each other.

I went to her and put out my hand to help her to arise, but she had scrambled to her feet awkwardly. I wished that she had allowed me to touch her. She was, after all, my only living relative besides Grandfather. I'd never had an aunt that I could remember. And there was something pathetic about that shriveled-apple face, in spite of its coldness. Perhaps she needed someone, too.

"Aunt Charlotte!"

I followed her as she backed away from me. Touched with pity for her I might be, but I was determined that I would say the things I had come here to say.

I began, "We must talk, dear. I must ask you certain questions and I want you to answer them."

The dull, hurting look in her eyes was gone now and I could see the fires of fear burning in them. "Why did you go upstairs yesterday?" she whispered. "You saw Craig!"

I had not meant to talk about Craig yet, but some of the questions were about him and so I said, "Yes. I saw him at his window one day and I wanted to know who was up there. Cieta told you, I suppose, that I visited Craig. Was that wrong, Aunt Charlotte? Shouldn't I have gone to his room?"

"She was furious. She was like a——like a

——" She broke off and looked fearfully at the door as though she expected to see Cieta somewhere in sight. "Oh, Alicia!" I heard Aunt Charlotte's voice break and I moved closer to her, but she waved me away. "You never should have come here, you and Jasper! You have made trouble for us. She will take it out on Craig!"

"But why? Who is he?" I spoke rapidly, my words cutting across hers, for her nerves seemed to be at the breaking point and I feared that she might become hysterical at any moment. "Why does he stay in his room all the time? He did not appear to me to be actually ill. What is wrong with him?"

She began to move her head from side to side. I captured her hands at last and she let them lie limp in my grasp, not seeming to know that I held them.

"Thomas was his uncle," she mumbled. "His parents were killed when their horse ran away and overturned the carriage. They died instantly but Craig, who was riding with them, escaped death. He——he was twelve at the time and he had no one else. It was ten years ago that I——" She drew a breath and then went on. "I had him brought here. There was no other place for him. He's been here ever since."

She tried to pull her hands away and she began to look about frantically, as though searching for an avenue of escape. But I held her firmly.

"That is who he is then. But what is wrong with him? Has he always been ill?"

She whispered, so low I could scarcely hear her, "No."

"Then why does he remain in bed? He can walk——he went to the window and looked out at me. He seems very intelligent. There is nothing wrong with his mind, is there?"

She shook her head without looking at me.

"A weak heart? A disease that keeps him debilitated?"

Again she whispered, "No. But he must—— he must stay there. Cieta——she takes care of him now. When he was younger I taught him his lessons. He was an apt pupil and we would read together. But no more. He is in her charge now. She keeps him——" She broke off suddenly and looked up at me with panic in her eyes.

"A prisoner? Aunt Charlotte, is Cieta in love with Craig? The way she looked at me when she found me with him——it was, oh, it was as though some terrible jealousy welled up in her that she could scarcely control! Does she love him? Is that it?"

"Yes!" The word burst from her lips. Her face grew flushed, as though with anger. "You have made me say it! Do not ask me any more questions, Alicia. It is better that you do not know any of these things. Believe me, it is better!"

I persisted stubbornly. "How can she keep him a prisoner if he isn't actually ill? Why doesn't he assert himself? He is not——he is not in love with her, too, is he?"

"I can tell you nothing more. Oh, Alicia, please go away! Leave as soon as you can!"

Her words were almost the exact ones Dr. Bruce had used when he, too, had urged me to go away. The memory of him as he said them, the tone of his voice, the good, masculine odor about him, flowed over me again and I felt more than ever agitated.

"There is nothing I want so much as to get out of here," I said in a voice not quite steady. "For this place, the house, Cieta——all of it terrifies me. I did not lie when I said that someone——she, I think——tried to kill me. And I do not understand the strange power she seems to have over you and Julio and Craig. I would have left the morning after our arrival if Grandfather had been well enough to travel. Now that he is strong enough something has happened to him and I am afraid of upsetting him. Aunt Charlotte, he is like a child! He talks of nothing except the past, seems to have gone back to the days when he lived here as a boy. I do not know what to do, for he becomes disturbed when I speak of leaving!"

Her face had begun to quiver and then seemed to crumble completely. I saw the flood of tears that washed over her eyes. She stood blinking sightlessly at me for a moment or two and then groped her way to a chair and sank into it. She put her hands over her face and when she spoke, her voice was muffled.

"It is the curse of the Lawsons!"

I touched her shoulder. "What are you talking about?"

It took me a little while to soothe her into calmness so that she could tell me what she meant. Between gulping sobs she said that all the Lawsons, her father and her grandfather, whom she remembered only dimly, had spent their last years in mindless babbling.

"The brain surrendered first to old age. It grew worse and worse until they died as unaware as they had been when they were born. I have seen it happen twice before. Now it is my brother—poor Jasper!"

She looked up. The creases and wrinkles of her face had been watered by her tears. I wanted to take her into my arms and comfort her, but I was afraid that any gesture of affection would bring on a total collapse. And so I spoke to her briskly as I got her to her feet.

"I must go to the village and see Dr. Bruce. If I tell him what has happened to Grandfather, perhaps he will have some suggestions to offer, some medicine that will sustain Grandfather until we get to Boston. And while I am in Seamount I can find out about train departures. How can I get to the village, Aunt Charlotte? You see I know nothing about hitching up a wagon; I have never driven a horse in my life."

"I will have Julio take you." She seemed to brighten a little. "We will not even have to keep it from Cieta. She will be glad to know that you are going away."

I asked sardonically, "She will give permission?"

Aunt Charlotte did not even notice the tone of my voice. She said earnestly, "I'm sure she will not object," with no explanation nor apology for the fact that it was Cieta who ruled the household and made the decisions in it. Again here was evidence of the dark-skinned girl's strange power at Blacktower. I wanted to ask Aunt Charlotte what the secret of that influence was, but I was afraid of bringing on another session of weeping which would delay me. I was anxious to be away, to take the first steps that would free Grandfather and me from Blacktower.

I said only, "Please keep an eye on Grandfather for me, Aunt Charlotte. You will not let anything happen to him in my absence, will you?"

She promised, with the stubborn look of purpose I had seen on her face once before, that she would watch over his safety. I felt cheered by that and my spirits lifted. Too, I would be seeing Dr. Bruce again. I felt almost light-headed at the prospect.

He had never seen me at my best. On those other occasions when we had met, I had been either bedraggled and travel-stained or somber with worry about Grandfather. And so I chose carefully the costume I would wear into Seamount.

The one I finally selected was of apple-green serge, a two-piece suit with a high neck and double rows of velvet buttons marching up the length of the short, tight jacket. It had bands of matching velvet on the collar and a full, sweeping skirt. I fluffed my hair out around my face so that it would show to its best advantage under a velours sailor hat with a cockade ornament bristling from its side.

When I was ready I stood in front of the cloudy mirror above my washstand and looked at myself critically. Excitement and anticipation had brought high color to my cheeks and my eyes did not have their usual grave and thoughtful expression. I was closer to prettiness than I had ever been before.

And I was glad. Glad that Andrew Bruce would see me this way, not overshadowed by Cieta's flamboyant beauty nor as a colorless sickroom drudge. Feeling happier than I had in days, I went down to the side yard and waited for Julio to bring the wagon out of the stable.

It was a bumpy old vehicle and far from

comfortable. It was littered with scraps of vegetables in its enclosed space behind us and there was a faint film of grain and wisps of hay over everything. When Julio made his periodic trips to the village for supplies, he evidently did not bother to clean out the wagon carefully. His person was untidy, too.

We did not say a single word to each other during that five-mile ride. The smell which emanated from him——of the stables and of the soil and of his unwashed body——was unpleasant and I was glad that we were out in the fresh air. The day was clear and dry and the horse's hoofs threw up little clouds of dust. The ocean rumbled in the distance; there was the occasional chirping of a bird, and the wagon clattered and creaked. But except for those things there was silence.

We came upon a white farmhouse glistening in the sunlight. As we approached the village, the houses grew closer together——most of them small and square and box-like and without porches or any ornamentation. But some of them had beautiful fan-shaped glass over their doors and all had the neat, well-kept look of New England.

All of the village could be seen at a glance. It was built around a narrow park and dominated by a church with simple lines and a high spire thrusting upward toward the sky. We stopped at the edge of the little town where wooden steps led up to a general store.

Julio turned and looked at me, his black eyes bright and expectant. I guessed that he was waiting for payment of some sort, a tip. I opened my purse and took out a dollar bill. Before I had a chance to hand it to him, he had snatched it away from me. He did not wait to help me out of the wagon but jumped down and, without a backward glance, dashed in the direction of the store.

I had to climb down myself and find my way to the railroad depot. It was deserted except for the stationmaster who handed me, rather grudgingly I thought, a timetable.

Then I went in search of Dr. Bruce's house. It was not hard to find because a black and gold sign with his name upon it was thrust into the lawn in front of it. As I went in the direction of the steps, my heart began to beat more rapidly. Then it seemed to stop, hung suspended for a moment without moving. For the door opened and Andrew came out.

CHAPTER SIX

He had a small black bag in one hand and he had been hurrying, moving briskly toward the steps. But when he saw me he stopped and we stood staring at each other.

"Alicia!" I thought I heard glad surprise in his voice and then it became concerned and sober. "Is there something I can do for you? Your grandfather hasn't had a bad turn?"

"He is no worse. But there is something—— I would like to tell you about it, Dr. Bruce."

He said that he had been on his way to make a call in the country and that it was an important one that he could not postpone.

"Why don't you come along with me? It's a fair distance and you can be telling me about it, whatever you've come to say, on the way."

I think that I accepted the invitation with unseemly haste. But I was eager to be with him. We have never had the opportunity for leisurely conversation, and today he seemed more the way he had been when I saw him for the first time. There was solicitude in his manner as he helped me into the two-seated carriage which stood waiting in the side yard. He was careful of my comfort, wrapped the lap robe around my knees, made sure I was warm enough.

When we had left the village behind and began to wind through a rutted country lane, I described in detail the deterioration of Grandfather's mind and I explained my anxiety to get him back to Boston.

"That's the only reason you want to leave?" He turned and looked at me with an unfathomable expression in his eyes. "You seem nervous today, Alicia. Has anything been happening there at Blacktower?"

In the quiet of the countryside, with the sunlight filtering through the bony trees and throwing mottled patterns in our path, the events of those dark nights in the big house seemed faraway and unreal. I was afraid that he would laugh at me, consider me a twittering female if I told him about the things I had heard, that I feared for my life and Grandfather's.

And I could not tell him about Cieta, of her hatred for me and how I had incurred it, because I had sensed that he was attracted to her, and I shrank from sounding jealous-minded and petty.

"Oh, there are things," I said vaguely. "You said practically the same thing, Dr. Bruce. You told me we should get away as soon as possible. It is not our home, after all. We don't belong there."

He asked me how we had happened to come to Blacktower in the first place and I told him. He was silent for a long time and at last I ventured, a little chilled by his withdrawal,

"You have never told me why we should leave, the reason for your warning. It was a warning, wasn't it?"

He did not answer me, for he was pulling on the reins to make the turn on a path which led to an old farmhouse. He said, "This is where I have a patient. You do not mind waiting?"

I did not at first, but he was gone a long time and I began to feel chilled. Then, when he came out, he seemed preoccupied and sober. He did not speak as he got in beside me and drove the horse back down to the narrow road.

It did not seem as though he intended to speak to me at all. We simply sat there side by side without a word between us. Then he pulled on the reins abruptly and the carriage swayed to a stop.

I turned to look at him and found that he had moved closer to me. His arms moved and lifted to my shoulders and before I had a chance to catch my breath he had drawn me to him in a close embrace.

For a moment I was too astounded to do anything except stare into the face close above mine. My eyes looked into the brown depths of his. What I saw there, the warmth and the ardor, made my heart race even faster until I could scarcely breathe.

My mouth moved toward his lips and he covered it with a hard and demanding kiss. My excitement died, drowned by a warm tide of happiness which surged throughout me. I knew I belonged there in Andrew's arms, that I had always wanted this, that there would never be another moment of such pure joy.

I felt as though all my senses had left me, yet I was aware that my lips were pressing against his with responding ardor. My arms had lifted and wrapped themselves around his neck; I was holding his head down to me; my fingers were lost in the soft hair at the base of it.

He made the first move to break the embrace. He lifted his face away from mine and although I whispered, "Andrew! Andrew!" with my lips seeking his, he gently disentangled my arms.

That brought me back to my senses with a shock. I slumped back against the seat, appalled now at my unmaidenly behavior. To have kissed a man in that fashion was a wanton thing, at variance with my moral code and upbringing. That he had been stronger and more controlled than I shamed and confused me. My face was flaming as I turned away from him.

There was only one circumstance that would justify a passionate embrace of that sort. If he were to propose marriage to me, if I knew that I was to be his wife——

"Alicia!"

When I did not look at him, he put out his hand and clamped it over my chin and moved my face so that it was close to his again. Yet I could not meet his eyes. He began to speak in a voice that sounded harsh.

"I hope you will forgive me. I should not have done that. I knew that you were troubled, vulnerable. At a time like that, when all your defenses were down——"

As I realized what he was saying, everything inside me seemed to freeze and stiffen. He was making excuses for me, and he was apologizing. He was treating what had happened between us as something light and passing, something born of an impulse and soon to be forgotten.

I could say nothing. Anger was melting my chill. I groped for my handerchief and raised it to my lips and scrubbed them. I heard him sigh. Then he picked up the reins and called to his horse.

We had driven a little way down the road before he spoke again. "I am sorry, you know. I'd hoped that we could be friends."

Friends! Whenever I had dreamed of him all these weeks past, I had not thought of him as merely a friend.

"Your apology is accepted," I told him coldly. "Now if you don't mind, we'll let the matter drop. I don't want to talk about what happened, nor explain it nor belabor it. I'd just like to forget it."

But although I drew away from him, he took my hand and held it firmly, his fingers so tight that mine began to throb. "You have to let me tell you how sorry I am. It was a caddish thing to do. You came to me today to enlist my help and I should have kept that in mind. But there's a sweetness about you, an appealing sort of, loveliness, and it weakened me. And I'm afraid I have been of no help whatsoever. Yes, I can give you a pill that will quiet your Grandfather for a little while. As to the other things——" He began to shake his head. "There is nothing I can say right now. You see, I must not——"

He broke off abruptly. When he spoke again, his voice had changed.

"How is Cieta these days? What is she doing?"

I gasped as suddenly as though he had dashed a flood of cold water into my face as, indeed, I felt that he had. I could scarcely believe it. Only moments before he had held me in his arms, the heat of his lips had warmed my own. No more than a few seconds had passed since he had spoken of my "sweetness" and "loveliness" and sounded solicitous and concerned about me. My hand still tingled from his touch.

And now it was evident that he had been thinking all that time about Cieta!

My anger returned and mounted as I recognized his motives. He had hoped to put me in a softened mood by his kisses and hand-holding. But in his eagerness to talk about this woman with the strange, frightening power who had woven a spell about him, too, he had spoken too quickly. I was still too aware of him, too sensitive to everything he said and did.

And I was not going to let him "pump" me. That was the distasteful word that sprang into my mind. All doubt was gone now; I was certain that he was in love with Cieta. For what other reason would he have been glad to see me and invited me to drive out into the country except to learn more, at first-hand, about her?

Hurt myself, I wanted to strike back at him. I scarcely recognized my own voice, with the notes of malice in it, when I said, "Cieta would not be interested in you, Dr. Bruce. I know that she loves someone else. Mrs. Prescott has told me so. There is a young man, the nephew of her late husband. You spoke about him to me once. Cieta takes care of him although I suspect that he is not actually ill. Aunt Charlotte practically admitted that, too. But somehow——somehow——" my voice faltered, "Cieta manages to make him believe that he is sick. So that, I think, he will be dependent upon her."

He was very still and I could feel his gaze upon me but I could not force myself to look at him.

The moment I had finished saying the spiteful words I had regretted them. It was the first time in my life I had been deliberately cruel. In inflicting pain I had not alleviated my own. I had sounded shrewish and pettish and I wished that I could take back the words. Or at least say that I was sorry for having uttered them.

But pride kept me silent and I kept my eyes turned away from Andrew for fear that he would see in them my disappointment and pique. Nor did he speak again. We rode back to the center of Seamount like two strangers who find themselves together on a short journey.

When the carriage stopped he jumped out and came around to me and extended his hand to help me down. But I drew back from it and brushed past him, still without looking at him. If he had called me back, I think I would have stopped to listen to what he had to say, accepted any explanation he could have given me.

But he did not call and there was evidently no explanation, and so I walked ahead, my heart feeling bruised and raw, to where Julio stood beside the wagon in front of the store and waited for me. He was smoking a long, black cigar which had been bought, doubtlessly, with the money I had given him. Its odor mingled with the others about him as we drove back to Blacktower.

My thoughts were whirling now. Speaking of Craig and Cieta aloud a few moments before had brought them into my mind with force and now they possessed it. What I had said about her keeping him a virtual prisoner seemed like a clear-cut fact now.

Craig's face rose before me, boyish and appealing, and I was moved with pity for that young life wasted behind the walls of a sickroom.

It was unthinkable that he should languish there forever enslaved (that was the word that came to me) by this woman who evidently wanted to possess him body and soul. He was nothing to me except another human being.

And I knew then what I must do.

Now it was time for me to start making definite plans for taking Grandfather away from Blacktower. I had not had a chance to ask Dr. Bruce for pills or medicine to make the journey easier. But perhaps he could manage without them.

Our leaving would have to be secret, and that was the reason there must be thought and planning. We were not wanted at Blacktower. Aunt Charlotte had made that plain and my presence was so abhorrent to Cieta that she had evidently tried to kill me on the night of our arrival. She wanted to be rid of us one way or another. Yet she would never let us go if she knew what I planned to do.

For I knew that I would never be able to simply walk away and leave that helpless boy to the mercies of the woman who ruled the household and all its members. I would not be able to turn my back upon him feeling, as I did, that there was no reason for his being kept an invalid. I had to give him his chance to escape, too, and perhaps be cured of what I felt must be only a minor ailment if any at all. I had made up my mind.

When Grandfather and I left Blacktower we would take Craig with us.

CHAPTER SEVEN

Whether my motives were selflessly pure at the time, or if they were tainted by my jealousy of Cieta, I do not know. I still burned with humiliation because Andrew had let her possess his thoughts when all mine had been for him. Perhaps I was unconsciously seeking some sort of revenge upon her.

Yet whenever I thought of Craig my heart melted with pity. I convinced myself that what I would be doing was right. He must not be abandoned there in that small, cluttered room with only his books and his charts and the sight of the ocean beyond his window to lighten his long hours of confinement.

I had no idea how I would manage to get him and Grandfather away without Cieta finding out about it, nor how I would actually accomplish our going. Five miles, the distance from Blacktower to Seamount, was a long way to travel with a muddle-brained old man and a delicate boy.

And I was all too aware of the danger involved. If Cieta discovered my intentions she would not hesitate to kill me; I felt sure of that. There had been something savage in her face when she had discovered me in Craig's room the day before. She would kill without compunction if she must make the choice between murder and losing the one she loved.

If I died in that remote house which had no visitors and no communication with the outside world, the fact might never be uncovered. For Grandfather no longer seemed sure of who I was these days; the others, Julio and Aunt Charlotte and Craig, were too completely under Cieta's domination to bring punishment upon her.

The empty grave I had seen in the cemetery might contain my body before long. The thought petrified me.

My nerves were strung tightly by the time we reached the house. The horrible thoughts which had pressed upon me sped my feet as I rushed over the stairs and down the hall to Grandfather's room. Worry for him, fear that he might have to share whatever fate awaited me, came up into my throat in a hard lump.

I stopped at the threshold, seeing that he was not alone. Sitting on a chair drawn up close to his was Aunt Charlotte. Brother and sister were holding hands like children and their voices held bright, excited notes.

At all other times, on the few occasions I had spoken to Aunt Charlotte, she had answered me in near-whispers and little gasps. But now she talked in loud shrillness, although her head was bent close to Grandfather's in a conspiratorial way.

"Some day soon we will do it, won't we, Jasper?" She bounced lightly up and down, her fat little body jiggling. "When there is no one about. We'll sneak out before daylight, before Mother and the others are awake. We will explore the cliffs then. Do you think we'll be able to find the cave?"

"I have a good idea where it is." Grandfather's white-maned head moved in a nod. "I told you I found that old map in Father's study. It was unmarked——where the treasure was buried, I mean. We shall have to search, perhaps, for a long time. But I know it is there. We've heard the stories, both you and I, about how the pirates came up on the shore and hid their loot in the cave."

Then he added, warningly, "But you must be careful not to give our secret away. We don't want anyone to learn about it and Father would stop us if he knew what we were going to do."

"Oh, I will, Jasper!" she cried out. "I shall tell no one, not a single soul."

"He would be very angry," and Grandfather's voice seemed to grow troubled. "How many times has he told us to keep off the cliffs? He keeps talking and talking and talking about the danger of slipping and falling. I don't want Father to be angry with me again, Lottie."

I saw her pat the hand that held hers with her free one. She murmured something comforting to him but he thurst out his lip and made a childish grimace. That expression on his face told me that he had surrendered completely to his mental aberration. It both touched me and frightened me, and I could not hold back the exclamation that burst from my lips.

They started at the sound and looked up guiltily. They drew even closer together at the sight of me standing there. My heart had dropped when I realized what had taken place, and now it ached painfully. I had tried to believe at first that Aunt Charlotte was merely humoring Grandfather by playing his game of fantasy with him. But her eyes were upon me now and I saw that they were over-bright and that there was something wild in them. And I knew that it was no game.

Grandfather had drawn her back into the world of the past. Perhaps I had brought her to the breaking point with my insistent questions. At any rate poor, ravaged Charlotte, who patently lived with some torturing secret, had fled from it, let her mind run away from the present. I could have wept for her.

The guilty expressions remained stamped on their faces as they looked at me, and then gradually changed to resentment. I had spoiled their fun; I had interrupted their plotting and planning; I was the grown-up enemy.

Aunt Charlotte got up at last with a little flounce of her skirts. She tossed her head defiantly as she passed me on her way to the door. I stood and watched her go.

"The curse of the Lawsons," she had said.

Neither of us could have guessed that she would be its victim so soon.

As I bathed Grandfather and got him ready for his supper, my mind was absorbed with Aunt Charlotte. The two, brother and sister, had found a common meeting place at last, now almost at the end of their lives. I had seen the way they had clung together, fingers entwined, in need and search for comfort.

How could I separate them now, these two old people who had rekindled a special kind of love between them? It would be sheer cruelty, I knew, to take Grandfather away and leave Aunt Charlotte behind. For Cieta, finding Craig gone, might vent upon the helpless old woman her own fury. And in Cieta there was a cruelty I had glimpsed once. I suspected that she was murderous. And I feared that Aunt Charlotte, if she were left alone here, would be in peril.

I would have to take her with us. There would be one more passenger, another elderly child, on that journey.

My planning began, at that moment, to take definite steps. I would need a vehicle to take us to Seamount; that was the most important detail. Once there I might be able to enlist the help of someone if the need arose. Dr. Andrew Bruce? I dismissed him immediately from my mind. We had parted on unfriendly terms and I could not go to him and beg for assistance. Besides, I was certain that he was enthralled by Cieta. Had he not spoken of her too soon after our intimate moment of embracing? He might jump at the opportunity to thwart our leaving and thus gain her favor. I could not take that risk.

My mind returned to the vehicle I would need to transport us all. The farm wagon would serve, and I wondered if I could persuade Julio to hitch it up for me and about the possibility of his keeping our secret. I had sensed something greedy about him, and I remembered the way he had snatched the dollar bill from my hand when the wagon had stopped in front of the village store. He was my only hope.

The following day I visited Craig's room again. I waited until I heard the slamming of a door downstairs and then went to the side window in the hall. Once more I saw Cieta digging in the herb garden. As far away as she was, her figure diminished by distance, the sight of her unnerved me. But at least she was out of the house and I did not intend to remain on the fourth floor very long today. As quickly as I was able, I raced up the curving stairs.

Craig was lying flat in bed. His books and charts were scattered over the bedclothes, but he was doing nothing except staring at the ceiling. When I spoke to him he showed by no sign that he had heard me. His face looked closed and tight and unfriendly.

I said, "Craig, I hope I didn't get you into

any trouble the other day. Was she——was Cieta very angry with you? If so, I'm very sorry."

His eyes moved to my face and I was shocked by the look in them. They were dull glazed, dead-looking. He seemed like someone who had been beaten into hopelessness, and and anger, like a bright, licking flame, shot through me. What had Cieta done to him that he lay like a lashed animal, all like seeming to be gone from him?

I sat down beside him and touched his shoulder. "Please," I begged, "do not feel so badly. Things may be better soon. Perhaps before too long——"

Then I broke off before I finished what I had been about to say. For I realized that it would be folly to tell him what I was planning to do. If I failed with Julio, there was no other way to escape. I could not even be sure that Craig would want to go with us, but if he did and I offered him his freedom, it might be that I would be raising his hopes and then have to subject him to a bitter disappointment. It would be the cruelest thing I could have done to him.

He stirred finally and asked, "What do you mean, Alicia?"

I shook my head. "I will tell you some other time. There is not enough time now. For I mustn't stay too long. I don't want Cieta to come and find me here again!"

He pulled himself up on the bed. Now his eyes were no longer dull but bright, almost brilliant.

"You have seen her this morning? She has not been near me since I woke up. Did you see any signs of her coming here?"

What had brought him to life? Was it fear? Or was this strange love affair as one-sided as I had believed? His being in love with her would not be hard to understand. Seeing no one but Cieta, having her minister to him continually, he could have easily have become enthralled by her through dependency and proximity.

Impulsively I asked, "Craig, do you love Cieta?" not knowing why I let the words burst out and sorry the moment they were said.

His eyes became hooded again. He seemed to stiffen in affront, and I knew I had made a mistake in probing into his personal feelings when it was only the second time we had spoken to each other. I had thought of him often during the past hours and I had included him in my secret planning, and so he seemed close to me. But I was, after all, a stranger to him and I knew that I had offended him.

He said shortly, "No!"

In an effort to coax him back into friendliness, I began to tell him things about myself. I recounted my worry about Grandfather, revealed that I felt uneasy here in Blacktower (although I gave him no specific reasons for my malaise) and hinted that I would soon be leaving.

He listened to it all but I could not tell whether or not it diverted him. When I left the room he was lying as listless and lethargic as he had been when I entered it.

That little interlude with Craig made me more determined than ever that I would help him escape from Cieta. And I already knew what I must do about Aunt Charlotte.

I found her wandering around the house that day. She was humming nursery rhymes put to music and she moved with a light, bouncy step that was almost like dancing. I wondered what Cieta thought about the change in the other woman, but of course I did not have any way of knowing. For I saw her scarcely at all.

Deliberately, I managed to avoid face-to-face meetings by varied devious methods, not wanting her to see in my eyes that I was afraid of her, that I shrank from meeting those brilliant black eyes of hers with my own. I even feared that she had some strange power that would let her look into my mind and learn of the plot I was hatching. Thus had Blacktower affected me——I who had always prided myself on my good common sense!

Whenever I heard her footsteps coming up the staircase, I slipped out of Grandfather's room and into my own, pretending to be busy there while she served him his tray or dumped armfuls of fresh linen on his bed. When she came again to collect the tray, I would be in the bathroom letting the water rush out of the faucets loud and full so that she would believe that I was washing. I was rather cheered by my success with these little deceptions. Perhaps the things I must do to get us all out of Blacktower would not be so impossible after all.

Finally I went searching for Julio. I walked as far as the stable and entered the wide door. My nostrils became filled with the barn smells——dried hay and the horse's odor and mustiness. It was a spacious building but it held, in addition to the wagon I had ridden in with Julio, only two old uncared-for carriages which looked as though they had not been used for a long time. The horse was in a stall near the door, a mare so old and patient that I was emboldened to stroke her nose. I murmured to her, told her that she would be the means that would let me escape from this place, and that for that I would love her forever.

At that moment, I felt something cold touch my hand and I started in fright. My head seemed to turn of its own accord and I looked down. I saw that what had touched me was the nose of a great, sad dog with eyes hungry for affection. I stooped down and patted him and he nuzzled against me.

He looked neglected and unhappy, and I decided that he must be a stray. Certainly he was not a household pet here in Blacktower, for I had never seen him before nor heard his barking. There were burrs stuck under his chin and on the tender skin inside his ears, which led me to guess that he had been wandering around in the woods for a long time.

As gently as I could, I removed the burrs from the places where they would irritate him most. Together we went searching outside the barn until I found a covered pail containing what was evidently the discards of one of Julio's meals. I fed the scraps to the dog and he gobbled them up gratefully.

When he had finished eating, he cocked his head at me. Then he came over to me, wiggled into a sitting position and waved his paws in the air. I said, "Good doggie!" in applause for his little trick. I was sorry a moment later that I had encouraged him. He bounded in my direction and with a strong leap flung himself upon me with such enthusiasm that I almost toppled backward. This, I suppose, was an expression of gratitude, but I did not appreciate the imprint of his muddy paws on my chest.

He was still sitting on the grass in front of the stable, looking disconsolate and aggrieved, when I went again in search of Julio. He seemed to be nowhere in sight and I did not like to call out his name for fear Cieta would hear me.

There would be another time. I would have to curb my impatience, although that was not easy; although I told myself that with each passing day Grandfather's physical strength returned more and more, I could not be sure that his mind——and Aunt Charlotte's——would not deteriorate to such a degree that they would be helpless burdens and impossible to transport any distance at all.

From that moment on, I strained my ears for the sound of Julio's voice and his footsteps which I had come to recognize. But Cieta, as though by some instinctive perversity, went on caring for our needs.

And then, on a night at the end of another day of watching and listening for Julio, I was awakened by strange noises again. Once more I heard the clanging of a bell and, a little while later, the sound of muffled footsteps on the cliff. It was almost dawn; I could see the faint gray of it lightening my windows. The feeble light seemed to add eeriness to the dim noises. And I almost sprang from my bed when another sound, a high shriek of terror, split the air. Its shrillness lasted only a second and then it dwindled away in the distance.

I lay there huddling under the bedclothes for a little while longer, and then I got up. I seemed to be drawn, almost without will, in the direction of the door. My hands snatched at my bathrobe and I thrust my feet into my bedslippers. I ran to the sea-framing window of the hall and looked out.

All I knew was that I had to learn the secret of these strange sounds. This was the third time I had heard unexplained things going on.

I stood there with my eyes straining into the fading darkness. The clouds were still thick across a low, pale moon, but I could see lights glimmering mistily from far away. At last I was able to distinguish the outlines of a ship. It looked like an old-fashioned schooner with its four masts and their sails bobbing gently with the motion of the waves.

Had I raised the window and thrust out my head, I might have been able to see what was going on down there at the bottom of the craggy pile of rocks which stretched up from the ocean. But this might have attracted attention to myself. The sound of the old window lifting might be heard by someone I could not see but whom I knew to be there. Whatever was going on was being done in stealth, under cover of darkness as it had been done before. Someone, probably the same person who was out on the rocks now, had a secret to conceal. Was this the reason an attempt had been made to kill me, so that I would not learn that secret? If so, I was in even greater danger now that I had discovered more about what was going on.

Yet I knew nothing actually. And terrified as I was for my own safety and Grandfather's, the thought occurred to me that if I could act cautiously enough to learn that secret I would have a power of my own which I could put to use if the time ever came when I needed it.

Even more strongly now there pressed upon

me the sense of evil in the house, a feeling which had been vague and undefinable before but which seemed at this moment to become an ugly entity. I wanted to slink back into my room and hide from it. Yet I realized that I could not combat it until I knew what it was. I had to find out what was going on. For a little while I must conquer my fears.

There was only one place in Blacktower, I thought, where the cliff in front of it could be seen with unimpaired vision. I was not even sure I would be able to find access to the roof, but I had to try.

The second-floor hall was filled with shadows. In the dawning light, the red gas globe seemed dimmer than ever. I made my way on tiptoe to the foot of the staircase. An earthly silence seemed to hang over the house and the hall was full of grotesque shadows, the black woodwork and dark wallpaper looming on either side of me.

The stairs wound high above me, unfamiliar in the gloom and seeming more treacherous than at the other times I had climbed them. The prospect of going over all those curving stairs made me suddenly weak. I felt frozen with apprehension, all but my heart which was racing and thudding. Yet I forced myself to go ahead, up and up, past the third-floor landing and into the reaches of the top story.

There I stopped, not knowing where I would find the access, it there was one, that would lead to the roof. I went past closed doors, shutting behind them I knew not what. Except for the one which led to Craig's room, I had no idea what was here on this top story of Blacktower on the side of those doors. I tried to keep my footsteps quiet lest I awaken him from sleep, but haste pressed upon me and I ran along the hall with my eyes lifted to the ceiling.

At the very end of the corridor, close to the bulge which enclosed the tower, I saw a steep, ladder-like flight of stairs. I stopped there and saw that at the top of it there was an expanse of wood cut into the ceiling.

This, I could see, was the trapdoor to the roof.

I put my foot on the first rung of the crude staircase as cautiously as I could, but the old wood creaked under my weight. The sound was loud in the stillness and I halted, my throat constricted and dry, waiting to learn if it had been heard, if anyone would come to investigate the source of it.

Still nothing in the house seemed to move or breathe. It was like some great empty hulk that had been deserted by all living things. The silence seemed to throb around me and I moved slowly and carefully upward, all my senses alert with the feeling of impending danger. The air grew fetid until I could scarcely breathe. I was gasping by the time I reached the top of the ladder.

When I was within touching distance of the trapdoor, I put up my hands against it and shoved it with all my strength.

It was thick and heavy and I could move it only an inch or two. I tried again and then once more, and despair began to overwhelm me. I would never be able to move that barrier that kept me from the roof. Drawing long, ragged breaths, I heaved all my weight upward. Finally the board gave way and fell open with a clatter.

Again I waited to see if the sound had been heard and again could distinguish nothing in the thick silence. Then I pulled myself up through the opening and tumbled out on the tarred surface of the roof. I scrambled to my feet and ran in the direction of the ocean-side of the house. I clung close to the tower, hiding in its shadows, until I reached the turreted balustrade.

I could hear nothing now except the roaring of the waves. And as I looked down from the battlemented top of the house, disappointment plunged heavily inside me. I had been wrong. There was not an unobstructed view from this point. The cliff was hidden by one of the lower stories that jutted out and concealed the place where the rocks met the ocean.

All I could see was the dark expanse of the water with early-morning mists rising from it. The ship was still there, ghost-like and dim in the fog. Even as I stood there, it began to watched until it was gone and then, disappointed as well as exhausted from all my futile exertion, I started back in the direction of the trapdoor.

I stopped mid-way. Morning was breaking, the clouds tearing apart to reveal pale streaks of pink and blue and gold. I remembered that the north wall of Blacktower was sheer and unbroken by architectural embellishments. And I had never seen the entire estate nor much of the woods around. I turned and went to the other side of the roof and stood at the stone railing looking down and over the gardens, the outbuildings and the clearing at the edge of the small cemetery.

And, of course, my eyes moved to the graveyard itself. The stones were beginning to catch the first light of morning and they gleamed palely in uneven rows, Captain Lawson's tombstone looming larger even from this high, faraway spot. My blood seemed to freeze suddenly. There was a figure there among the graves. I could see it in motion. It bent, straightened up, and bent again. There was a steady rhythm about the movements and I could see, at regular intervals, the flash of something bright: something which rose and fell and was lost to sight in the earth for a moment or two.

I could not have helped knowing what those motions meant. Someone was digging in the graveyard.

CHAPTER EIGHT

The sight of that busy figure in the cemetery both frightened and repelled me as nothing had ever done before. My first thought was that a plot was being prepared for burial. But one had been made ready. There had been that deep, waiting hole among the other graves which I had stumbled over only a few days before. The man at work out there might be filling in that pit after depositing a body in it.

Whose body?

My teeth made a chattering noise as I scrambled down through the trapdoor and groped my way down the steep ladder of steps. I could feel my feet slither on the polished staircase. Once I came close to falling, but managed to grasp the banister and I clung to it as I made the twists and turns down to the second floor.

Then I stopped. For to my right was the tower wall and I could hear coming from behind it again the sounds of low, muffled moans. I was held there without the strength to move a step further. Those terrible noises seemed to rip at my heart and very soul. It was a chorus of misery from unknown throats. All the people who lived in the house, Cieta and Julio and Aunt Charlotte, could not have raised such a clamor of distress. I guessed that there were at least six voices.

And I was almost certain now that whatever was going on behind the tower wall was the heart of the mystery. Something so vile and unspeakable that the arrival of two outsiders, Grandfather and me, had thrown Aunt Charlotte into a panic and made her urge me to leave the house. Something so evilly secret that Cieta had wanted me dead rather than run the risk of my learning of it.

A picture of Cieta rose in my mind, and it was almost as though she were standing there, her black eyes glittering at me, her gaze searing me. Where had she been for the past hours that she did not know that I was abroad, had not heard me running over the stairs and through the halls?

The power I suspected she possessed——the power to keep people enslaved and helpless against their wills——would it not let her know where I had been, what I had been doing? I began to tremble then so that I had to cling to the swirled top of the newel post to hold myself erect.

Even the thought of Cieta, the memory of her arrogant, inscrutable face, could do this to me.

There was nothing I now wanted so much as to reach my room, the only haven I had in this great house of evil shadows, and lock the door behind me. My throat ached from my dry gasping by the time I reached the end of the hall, and I went past Grandfather's open door without slowing down.

Open!

But his door was never left ajar at night. I had always made sure that it was closed tightly after our first night at Blacktower least he be awakened by unfamiliar noises and become disturbed by them. I had done that tonight, had pulled the knob of the door after me carefully as I left him asleep; I had heard the click of the latch.

I stopped short and turned. There was a cold, prickling sensation running along my arms and legs and spreading to my fingers and toes. I could scarcely force myself to walk back to the open door. I was sick with dread and premonition when I looked in through it.

The window was gray with its veil of feeble dawn light and the furnishings in the room loomed like faint shadows. The bed drew my eyes and I tried to tell myself, when the menacing horror became a fact, that they must be playing tricks on me.

It was not a trick of vision. It was not imagination. The bed was empty.

"Grandfather!"

The word came surging up into my throat and burst through my lips in a thin squeak. In that moment when my fears that he was not in his room were confirmed, my heart had seemed to stop. Now it came to life again and it began to beat hard and heavy.

I seized upon the thought of the bathroom. Until now I had always helped him when he wanted to go to the little room opposite the hall from us. But might he not have decided, upon waking up during the night, to venture that far under his own power? And collapsed there to lie helpless until someone came to find him?

He was not in the bathroom. Nor in my bedroom. Nor in either his closet or mine. Frantic with fear, I sped from one door to another down the hall, wrenching them open and looking into them quickly. There was not much light yet; still, I would have found him if he had been in any of those rooms.

There were a great many of them—I did not take the time to count. In one of them I found Aunt Charlotte, her face soft and gray in sleep. Her fist was under her cheek and her hair hung in long braids over the bedclothes. She did not awaken when I went in to look down at her.

Now I did not care who heard me as I rushed from place to place, searching. I cried out from time to time, "Grandfather!" The word seemed to echo back at me from the corners of the rooms and along the stretches of the corridor.

When I reached the end of the hall, close to the tower wall, I could hear the voices. They were fainter now, scarcely audible, but I no longer cared about them. All that concerned me was finding Grandfather before some harm befell him. He was not physically strong enough to have walked far nor mentally capable of wandering about in the dim light of this big house.

Because of course he must be in the house. There was no other explanation that my mind would accept. He had awakened, decided to explore parts of Blacktower that he remembered and had not seen since he was a boy. I would not——could not——let myself believe that his absence was due to any other circumstance.

I did not even consider going up to the third and fourth floors. For I could not imagine how Grandfather, his legs still weak and uncertain from his illness, could have managed to climb any of those steps of the winding staircase. He might have made his way to the first floor; that would be easier than climbing upward. And so I ran down there, when my search of the bedrooms was finished, and began it again in the kitchen.

There was no light in it, for the trees and shrubbery beyond its windows threw a curtain of darkness over them, and the great tables and stoves looked like shapeless figures in the shadows. Grandfather was not there.

The halls, the long front one and the other one leading from the butler's pantry were empty. The double doors of the other rooms at the front of the house—I had so far only glimpsed the dining room and parlors—were securely locked.

I thought of Captain Lawson's study. Perhaps it had been a favorite spot of Grandfather's when he was a boy; any child would have been fascinated by the ship models and the scrimshaw articles and the curios. I wondered why I had not thought of that room before this.

The door of the study was unlocked but it, too, was empty. And I could not think of anyplace else to search. I had not found Grandfather in any of the places in the house that seemed likely.

Surrounded by the treasures of the man who had built Blacktower, not seeing them or aware of their beauty, I was suddenly overwhelmed by the dreadful thoughts which I had been pushing out of my mind for the past hour. Now they clamored insistently to be heard.

The significance of what I had seen in the cemetery coupled with Grandfather's disappearance added up to something so horrible that I put a hand over my eyes as though I could shut the picture out of my brain. Somebody had tried to kill me. Why not Grandfather, too, if he had somehow discovered something that someone was desperate not to have known?

I was sick with horror and guilt. I had left the helpless, confused old man alone while I was poking about in the high reaches of the house and gawking from the turreted roof. If anything had happened to him, I would hold myself to blame. It was not inconceivable that he had gotten out of bed and wandered out into the hall and seen something he was not supposed to have seen. There was another reason, too, that his life could be in peril. I must have known it all along and yet refused to acknowledge it.

There was the money. Grandfather was an heir to the Lawson fortune. Murder and greed, I had read somewhere once, go together. And that would point to only one person. But Aunt Charlotte was in her bed sleeping serenely. Not, surely, after having killed her brother?

I did not know what I would find in the cemetery nor how I would learn whose body was buried under the fresh mound of dirt. But I felt impelled to go there since there was nothing for me to do here in the house now that I had become certain that Grandfather was nowhere in it.

My frantic thoughts moved to Julio. He was the only one I had to turn to and I was desperate. I would promise him anything— anything at all——if he would tell me what he knew about my grandfather's disappearance.

I ran upstairs and grabbed at the first dress that came to hand, exchanged my bedslippers for sturdy shoes and threw a cloak around me.

The side door was, fortunately, unlocked and I ran through it and down the stone terrace and onto the narrow path that led past the outbuildings. The earth was soft and damp under my feet and the morning air was chill. Yet there burned inside me a fever. I came to the barn and threw myself upon its door, crying out Julio's name. He did not answer me at first and I beat my hands upon the wooden surface until they became sore.

Then finally he came and slid back the door and stood looking at me with his small, black beads of eyes. He wore a full-sleeved blouse, faded and wrinkled, and trousers that were shiny with grease and age. He stood blinking into the light with a dazed and stupid expression on his face. I knew that I had awakened him and that he wore the same clothing by night and by day, even when he was in bed.

"What you want? What you want?" He sounded angry and not, I thought, simply because I had disturbed his sleep. "You got no right to be here."

My voice was shaking as I told him about Grandfather's being missing. His thin shoulders moved in a shrug. "Thees I do not know about. I do not see heem."

"But you will help me find him? Julio, please! I want you to go with me to the cemetery. We can begin to look for him there."

He made a backward movement, a sudden, jerking motion of his body that was like cringing. Fear flamed in his eyes for an instant and then he put his hand on the door and I knew

115

that he intended to close it in my face. My speaking of the cemetery had terrified him. Perhaps ignorance and superstition made this uneducated man fearful of the dead. Or perhaps he had some guilty knowledge of what had taken place there in the graveyard that night. He might not be frightened so much of the dead who rested there as of one living person——Cieta.

I had seen both hatred and submission in his face when she had given him his orders. Now perhaps even the thought of her was making him stare with fright and clutch at the door jamb in a spasm of shivering.

"Julio," I begged again, "you must know something, have heard something. If you will help me——if you will tell me what you know——I will pay you when I can. I have no money with me now, but I promise I will give you some if you will come with me to the graveyard."

His face became a battleground of expressions. I knew that he was being torn between his greed and his fear. The little black eyes gleamed and glistened but his lips fell back over his teeth like those of a cornered animal. He began to shake his head.

"I do not do thees thing you want. You go away now. Eef she find you here——"

His hands made shooing motions as he darted a glance in the direction of the house. I went on trying to plead with him but he would not listen.

"Go away! Queeckly please! She be very angry. You do not know what she do!"

He stepped back into the barn and closed the door. I stood there with tears of frustration and despair spilling down my cheeks. If Julio would not help me now, when I had wanted him only to go with me to a place a few feet away, it was ridiculous to hope that I could bribe him to loan me the horse and wagon.

Feeling shattered by desolation, I walked blindly back to the path. Everything was a watery blur through my tears and I did not see where I was going. I stumbled over something in my path, plunged forward and felt the hardness of the earth against my body as I fell upon it. Shaken by my fall, I tried to struggle to my feet but something leaped upon me and held me on the ground.

I looked up into the hairy face of the stray dog I had come upon a few days ago. His paws pressed heavily on my chest and his long, moist tongue began to lick at my face. When I had shoved him aside and scrambled up off the ground, he began to bark joyously and throw himself at me as though this were some sort of game I had devised for his amusement.

"Go away! I don't want to play with you. Shoo!"

I made my voice sharp and stern and I tried to push him off me, but he had evidently

117

recognized me as someone familiar in his friendless world. And even though I managed to escape from his paws and tried to hurry out of his reach, he loped along beside me yelping happily.

"Please!" I stopped finally and put a restraining hand on his head. "Won't you please be quiet? Fido? Rex? Rover?" I thought that if he heard his name he might feel impelled to obey. "Prince?"

His tail began to wag as I said that last name. Either it actually was what he was called by or else he liked its sibilance. The barking stopped but he began to dash around my legs, and I knew that I had to get rid of him. I had enough to burden me now without a stray dog tagging after me. He might become noisy again at any minute and thus attract attention to me. I had been lucky so far and I did not want to take any more risks of being discovered.

I found a stick on the path and held it to the dog's nose for a moment so that he could smell it. Then I lifted my arm and threw it as far as I could. It landed somewhere in the shrubbery and he went racing after it, his powerful body shattering the twigs of the bushes as he went with a sound like a series of pistol shots.

Now that I was free of him, I hurried forward, crossed the clearing and came into the graveyard. With the brightening of the day Captain Lawson's tombstone and the smaller ones around it had grown whiter than when I had seen them from the roof. It came to me suddenly what I was doing.

I was standing in almost the same spot where someone had been digging——or filling in a grave——only a short time before. Here among the remains of my ancestors and the servants who had worked at Blacktower and the strangers whose graves were unmarked, I was alone and unprotected. The person with the shovel could not be far off.

But there was no one in sight, not on any of the paths nor behind the stones which I passed cautiously on my way to the spot where I had seen the empty hole.

I stopped at a point a foot away from it. The pit no longer yawned. It had been filled in, as I had suspected, and a mound of fresh dirt was humped over it. Fresh black dirt which had not become dried by the sun, moistened by rains or overgrown with any sort of plant life.

There could be no doubt about it. A burial had taken place here recently.

Certain of that now, I had no idea of what my next steps would be. I had no way of knowing whose body had been placed beneath that fresh mound of dirt. I could not allow myself to believe that it was Grandfather's, not even with all my fears.

Even while I tried to cling to hope, a spasm of weeping shook me again. And my mind became a squirrel cage of questions.

What could Grandfather have learned, what could his befuddled mind have grasped? Could it really have been Aunt Charlotte who had wanted him out of the way, killed him herself or had someone do it for her? I could not believe that there was violence hidden under that soft, bewildered exterior. The curse of the Lawsons was not blood lust but a deterioration of the mind.

Still, he had never left his room since our arrival at Blacktower until tonight, had displayed no curiosity about what was going on in it——

The thought was never finished, for I felt a sudden burst of pain at the back of my head. A million pinpoints of light exploded in my brain. And then blackness overcame me.

CHAPTER NINE

I do not know how long I lay there unconscious. When my eyes finally opened, their lids feeling heavy and sore, I looked up into the sky and it appeared to be lighter and its colors had deepened and grown brighter. I had grown chilled, although I could feel something weighty upon me. The cold seemed to have seeped into every part of my body so that even my bones were aching.

There was a low moaning sound in my ears and it took me a moment or two to realize that it was my own voice I heard. And then I became aware that my head was being lifted gently and that fingers had begun to explore the back of my skull. I turned my head too quickly and groaned as a lance of pain shot through it.

"Lie still, Alicia. Let me move you when it's necessary."

I was not sure, at first, that I was not hearing that remembered voice in a dream. And then, as he lowered me back down on the ground, I saw Andrew Bruce's face come into view. It looked very grave and, I thought, a little angry.

"Do you want to tell me what happened,

Alicia? Don't overexert yourself, but just a few words?"

I closed my eyes quickly. His fingers were moving swiftly and skillfully over my head and face in search of injuries. I could not control the leap of my pulses. My senses seemed to come alive at his touch, and I was afraid that he would know of that warm, flooding emotion that had begun to surge over me.

"It was nothing," I murmured for he was still waiting for my answer. "I am all right."

"All right!" He repeated the words in a little yelp. "I find you here at dawn unconscious and half-frozen. And you tell me it's 'nothing'! Alicia, tell me the truth. What are you doing here? What happened to you?"

Still without looking at him, I said, "I awoke early and decided to go for a walk. I must have stumbled over something and hit my head when I fell. For that's all I remember——only the fall. I think I had better get up now."

"That's what you think?" His hand on my shoulder held me down. "I'll tell you when you can get up, young lady. And it won't be until I've got the whole story. You say you fell. Backwards? How could you have fallen backwards with enough force to bring a lump that size on your skull?"

"There was a dog."

I seized upon that half-lie, remembering that there actually had been poor Prince who had gone galloping into the woods after the stick I had thrown for him. But before that I had stumbled over him. And if there had been a rock on the path I might have bumped my head against it. So it was not an outright lie.

"He was big and strong," I mumbled. "He had great heavy paws and he knocked me off my feet."

Of course Andrew did not believe my story. I could sense that, even though I kept my eyes shut and did not look at him. I knew that he had stiffened and was kneeling there staring into my face in disbelief and anger that I had lied to him.

"For heaven's sakes, Alicia!" He seemed to grow impatient with me. "Going for a walk at this hour of the morning! And of all places— the cemetery! What would bring you to this place at dawn?"

I came very close to telling him. I was weakened by the shock of the attack upon me. My sore head and the chill that was almost like another pain inside me had torn down all my defenses. This above all things I wanted— to creep into Andrew's arms and pour out everything: my fears for Grandfather, my suspicions about the new grave, the strange things that were happening at Blacktower, the fact that someone had tried to kill me.

I longed for the strength of his arms and the comfort of his shoulder. But then he asked again, "What were you doing here, Alicia?" and the question echoed in my brain and reversed itself.

It came to me suddenly that I should be asking him the very same thing.

What was he doing here? His office was five miles away. Even if he had been summoned out on a house call to somewhere not too distant, Blacktower was a long way from the road to the village. No one here, I was sure, had summoned him to make a sick visit. What had brought him here, to this remote place, at the beginning of a new day?

Not "what" but "who". Who but Cieta? I could feel my face grow stiff when the answer came to me. For I remembered that I had not seen her all through the past night and that I had wondered about it. If she and Andrew had had a rendezvous, it would account for her not having been anywhere in sight.

Busy she might have been but not, it was evident, too busy for Andrew.

Now my face was flaming as I pictured them together. In one of the rooms I had not searched? Or did they hold their clandestine meetings in one of the outbuildings? The last seemed more logical. If Andrew had been stealing away in the first light of morning, he might have seen me lying here and, as a doctor, not been able to go away and ignore me.

I pushed away the heavy article that covered me as I forced myself into a sitting position. And I saw that it was his ulster and noticed for the first time that he wore only the jacket of his suit.

"You are in danger of catching cold," I said stiffly. "I am quite all right now, Dr. Bruce. Thank you for your concern and care."

He helped me to my feet and for a moment I swayed dizzily. His arms went around me and held me, and I was too weak and shaken to push him away.

He asked softly, "Is that all you have to say to me, Alicia?"

My vision cleared as I looked up at him. I thought I saw something tender and beseeching in his eyes, but the picture of him and Cieta together still possessed my mind. I would not let myself be affected by that glowing light. Nor by his next urgent words.

"If you would only tell me the truth of what happened! There may be some way I can help you."

"There is nothing. Please let me go!"

His arms fell away. "As you wish. But I think I should see you later today. There is no concussion, as far as I can determine, but you may be uncomfortable for a little while. You must go to bed immediately and rest for a few hours. I will look in upon you——"

"No!"

It was, I was sure, merely a ruse, an excuse to come to the house once more and see Cieta. I would not be a pawn in his devious, love-sick game.

"Do not come!" I said bluntly. "I would prefer that you did not."

He stepped forward and put his hand on my arm, whether to remonstrate with me or attempt to walk back to the house with me I did not know. At any rate, I shook off his grasp and turned away from him, angry and hurt.

I knew how graceless I must have looked lying there on the ground. The clothes I had thrown on hastily when I went in search of Julio had not been chosen for their attractiveness but merely because they had been handy. They had become rumpled and bedraggled, and my hair felt tossed and untidy. Yet Andrew, had I given him any encouragement, would have made love to me once more.

No doubt he had had an ulterior motive. Or perhaps he was one of those men who must exert their charms on all women, not seeing them as young or old, plain or beautiful, but merely as means of catering to their own vanity.

I did not intend to be one of those women. Andrew Bruce's blandishments would not work on me. I did not want attention and soft words from a man whose mouth might tingle with the kisses of another woman.

Although my back was turned to him as I went in the direction of the path, I knew that he stood there watching me. I was determined to put him out of my mind and I did; but then all the horror of Grandfather's being missing flowed over me again.

There was a narrow lane running between the stable and a storage shed; beyond it was the strip of green sea I could see from that point and the constant sound of the water. I stood there with my eyes turned in that direction, but I saw nothing, heard nothing.

I thought only of Grandfather. I could not believe that he had been taken from me, that I would never see him again. There could not be such an abrupt end to the companionship we had shared for so many years. He had been the moving force in my life since the day I went to live with him. My first thoughts on arising every morning had been for him. His comfort, his health, his welfare, had absorbed me.

Something other than death must have happened to him. In my imagination I saw him wandering around in the woods that stretched around Blacktower. To have attempted to search them all would be useless. And then I thought of the cliffs.

Not long ago I had heard someone speak of the cliffs, but the memory of what had been said flitted just out of reach of my mind.

And then, finally, I remembered; I heard Aunt Charlotte's voice talking about some sort of cave on the cliffs. She and Grandfather had talked of "buried treasure"; they had made plans to explore the cave together.

Grandfather had sounded as eager as a child on that day when I had found them together in his room. These days few things penetrated his brain or remained there if they did, but perhaps this talk of an excursion in search of pirate's gold had remained with him. He might have become confused over the difference between day and night and gone looking for the cave himself.

It was possible that he was still there, digging among the rocks, so engrossed with what he was doing that he had not been aware of his weakened condition and not known of the passage of time.

I seized upon that hope. I gave no thought to Andrew Bruce who might be still standing where I had left him. The path between the shed and the barn was so narrow that I had to squeeze my way through it. But that was a mere detail, nothing. Nor did I even think of the fact that he had ordered me to go to bed and rest. I would never be able to rest again until I found Grandfather.

From the barn on my right came the whinnying sound of the horse. I remembered that Julio was close by, but I was not afraid of the man-of-all-work. It was true that he had been unwilling to help me, but I was sure that he would not betray me to Cieta. He would not tell her that I had been roaming about in the cemetery, because when he had looked at her and later spoken of her, he had done so with bitter hatred.

Yet I went by the stable as quickly and quietly as I could. The dirge-like sound of the waves grew louder as I approached them; then it was there before me, that wild, tossing water that was now coming to its full tide. It climbed high on the rocks and left a shower of spray behind it.

I stood for a moment where a wall of stone fell straight down in a sheer drop. On both sides of me, along the coastline, the rocks formed craggy patterns by thrusting themselves out unevenly over the shore. At one point, where Blacktower rose up over the sea, there was a small crescent of sand. It was not even the tiniest beach and now it was being devoured by the waves that gobbled it up and then fell back to leave a lacy layer of foam at its edge.

A small boat might have been able to make its way through the rocks and beached on the sandy expanse. I guessed that this was the place where passengers had come ashore on three different nights. The rocks above it looked treacherous, yet not actually impossible to climb. But a misstep could be fatal and I remembered the terror-filled scream I had heard early that morning, the shriek that had petered out and died as the owner of the voice slipped off the rock and plunged downward. I knew that was what had happened; I was certain of it now.

Here, too, was the explanation of the new grave. There could have been other deaths in that or some other manner. It would account for the unmarked graves in the cemetery.

It was a horrible thought, yet I felt heartened. If my reasoning was true, it was not Grandfather who had been buried in that waiting pit and there was a good chance that I could find him alive. I had no idea where to look for the cave but I supposed it must be somewhere on the north side of Blacktower where the rocks jutted out with concealed places between them.

Below me was a narrow ledge, scarcely wider than my feet, which led past a formation of boulders. I lowered myself down onto it and then inched along it. I was afraid to look down at the water which swirled and climbed beneath me and I was still somewhat weak and dizzy from the blow on my head.

At the end of the ledge a huge boulder formed a barrier to my progress. I had to go down and around it, using the uneven surfaces of other rocks as steps. My trailing skirts, grown heavy with dampness, were hampering but I was thankful for the stout boots which were serving me well.

The rocks were slippery from the spray which rose high into the air and I felt my foot slither as I put it down on a narrow, uneven. surface. If I hadn't grasped at the point of a rock above me, I should have gone plunging down over the ragged stones and into the water. I held on tightly, the crag biting into my hand so sharply that I could feel pain shoot along my arm. But I held on until I regained my footing and then I crawled around the boulder.

It was no wonder, I thought, that Captain Lawson had forbidden the use of the cliffs as a playground for his children. They would have been taking their lives in their hands every time they went over this dangerous route. But there must be an easier access to the cave. It was ridiculous to think of Grandfather reaching it by this means. He must have known of another way; children would have a secret path——no doubt much less precarious than my own.

I found the cave a half-mile or so from the house. It was a natural formation in the rocks and above it a point of land stretched out like a platform. If I had known, I could have undoubtedly found that point by continuing on the road beyond the cemetery. That must have been the way Grandfather and Aunt Charlotte had approached it. Two flat stones even formed a staircase down into it.

As I stood at its mouth for a moment, breathless and exhausted from my climbing, I wondered if anyone had been in this place since the days Aunt Charlotte and Grandfather had explored its depths. It seemed odd that they would have both remembered it, even through the clouds in their minds; remembered it and spoke of it with gentle yearning.

The pirate's gold, I realized almost immediately, had been nowhere except in their childish imaginations. For it would have been impossible for anyone, even the bold adventurers they had fashioned in their minds, to have dragged treasure chests up that steep expanse of rocks.

Nor was the cave large enough for an adult person to stand erect. I had to crawl on my hands and knees through its opening. The dark interior smelled of old damp dirt and salt, and the sound of the wind and the ocean was a faint roar, the sort you can hear when you hold a conch shell to your ear.

There was no one in the cave, of course. I had seen that in a single glance. Nobody could have squatted in chill and discomfort there for very long. My dangerous undertaking had been futile, just as all my efforts to find Grandfather for the past hour had been useless. The house, the cemetery, the cave——what was left?

Only the far-flung forests and the grounds around Blacktower I had not yet explored. There were too many places to search and I wished now I had not rejected so flatly Andrew's offer of help. I thought of him with a heavy, painful longing, no longer picturing him as Cieta's lover but someone who might share my burden with his strength.

I was tired and chilled and yet I knew that I must go on. And so I crawled out of the cave and climbed the stones that led to the point of ground above them.

Which way should I start? I stood uncertain for a moment and my eyes moved in both directions. They fell upon Blacktower and my gaze remained riveted there.

Distance made it look smaller and the mists that enveloped it gave it an appearance of unreality, like something seen in a dream. The outlines of its turreted top were dim, but the tower itself was discernible as it rose high in the air like some symbol of evil. That was how I thought of it now, that dark cylinder looming against a lightening sky. The great hulking house which had seemed, a moment ago, like something in a dream now looked to me like part of a nightmare.

The tower—which had disturbed me with its ugliness at my first sight of it—looked more than ever like some horrible bastion where prisoners were held to languish and die. There spread over me a strange feeling as though the stones of the tower were falling away and I could see Grandfather held there behind them.

Where else could he be? I knew that I had to get into the tower somehow and look for him.

CHAPTER TEN

A narrow path led past a barrier of dark trees on my left. To the right was the cliff and there was scarcely enough room to walk between the two. I went along cautiously, controlling my haste and impatience, for this was unfamiliar territory and there were places where the lane curved and hid what was ahead.

I felt surer of myself when I reached the graveyard, and I tried to hurry past it. But my skirt was wet and heavy, and my shoes, sodden and muddy as they were, seemed to sink into the ground.

Just before I reached the herb garden I slowed down and gazed ahead. I was terrified of meeting Cieta. Weak and tired, I would be no match for her if she tried to kill me again. Danger seemed to lurk on all sides of me.

The north wall of Blacktower stretched up in front of me. I let my eyes travel its length and then rest on the window where I had seen, on that other day, Craig watching me through a telescope. Now there was no one there or at any of the other windows. They were empty but they gleamed like malevolent eyes.

The house itself seemed strangely still. With the secrets it held——the nighttime activities around it, voices of unknown people in its tower, the woman who ruled it with some evil and unexplainable power——it seemed as though it should bear some mark of infamy upon it. There it was, hulking and ominous-looking on this new morning. I shivered as I came abreast of its front entrance, and I fled past it as quickly as I could, slowing down only to look for the path which curved around it to the cliff.

The tower thrust itself out from the rest of the house on a platform of rock. The path became lost. There was only a small space between the cliff and the tower door, a great, heavy portal with an iron latch and hinges grown rusty from the rains and the salt air.

I put my hand on the latch with not very much hope that it would lift out of place. But it did. The door was not locked. It fell open when I pushed it.

This was something I had not dared to hope for. I had known that I would never be able to gain access to the tower through the inside of the house. Whenever I had seen the door near the front entrance, a heavy iron bar had lain across its lock. I had simply gone to the ocean side of the tower on the slimmest hope that I would find some way of getting into it.

As I went in cautiously, a fetid smell of dankness assailed my nostrils. The darkness blinded me momentarily. I could see nothing in the murky interior. Then my eyes grew accustomed to the gloom and I could make out the outlines of the winding stone steps that curved up and up until they became lost to view.

I moved toward them and stumbled over something at my feet. I looked down and saw that it was Grandfather lying there, limp and motionless like a bundle of old clothes, only his face shining palely in the dusk.

"Grandfather!" I cried out to him softly and fell on my knees beside him. I saw that he was wearing his heavy coat over his nightshirt and that his feet and legs were drawn up under it. His arms were held tightly to his sides, his hands clenched.

When I tried to lift him up, he whimpered something I could not understand and tried to pull away from me. Whatever had filled him with fear was still with him and I knew that he was struggling against something unknown.

"It's all right, Grandfather," I told him soothingly. "It's Alicia. I'm with you now. Let me help you up. You must come back to the house, back to bed."

All that concerned me at that moment was his well-being. I could not guess what effect lying in this cold, damp place might have on him.

When I finally got him into a sitting position, his pale eyes stared into mine blindly. I could see little in that half-dark place, but I was able to tell that his expression was blank and unaware. Whatever had sent him out into the darkness was not clear to him now. Only his fright remained. He was weak and confused and yet he had some instinctive need to keep his fist clenched to hide whatever he was holding in his hand.

"Let me have it, Grandfather!" I spoke firmly, as one might to a child in a demand for obedience. "Give me whatever you have there."

His fingers loosened and I saw gleaming in his palm a rusty key. And I knew that this was the key that had opened the tower door. I guessed that he had kept it all these years, hoarded it against the time when he would return to Blacktower and the places he had known as a child. Perhaps his talk with his sister had brought back those memories and he had become so possessed by them that he had not been able to resist the temptation to visit the tower. Or he might have heard the same sort of noises I had heard on three different occasions and, lucid for a short period of time, decided to investigate them for himself.

Whatever his reasons were for being there, I knew I had to get him out of there as quickly as possible. I tried to help him to his feet.

"You must come with me now, Grandfather. You might have caught a bad cold. We don't want you sick now, do we? For soon we are going to take a journey——"

When I saw the effect my words were having on him, I stopped speaking. His mouth began to move in spasms of agitation. His eyes blinked at me and then filled with water. He began to weep, poor unhappy Grandfather, in the thin, broken sobs of a baby.

It took me a little while to quiet him. But even after his crying had ceased, he would not let me take him away. There was something he tried to tell me, but at first he could not speak and stood gulping so that his Adam's apple bobbed up and down his veined neck.

Finally, when he had regained his self-control, I saw that his crying had had one good effect. It seemed to have broken away the mists of his confusion and his mind had become astonishingly clear. He spoke to me in the lucid, authoritative way I had not heard him use for a long time. He was more like himself than he had been for months.

"I do not wish to leave," he said, his voice low but firm. "I cannot go from here now. And not, certainly, from Blacktower until I learn what is going on. Alicia, there is a strangeness in the house. I have been aware of it, from time to time, ever since we came here. It is something I do not understand, but I shall get to the bottom of it."

His eyes were bright now, alert and with lights of wariness in them.

"Tonight I heard strange sounds. They awakened me and I went to look for you but you were not in your room. So I decided to find out for myself what was going on. Alicia, it is not right that there should be secrets kept from me. I am the master of Blacktower now that my father is dead. In spite of the way we parted, he would want that."

I feared for a moment that his enthrallment with the past was overtaking him once more. But even with his hair tousled and in his nightshirt, there was a sort of pride and dignity about him.

"Lottie is——is——" He shook his head in a troubled way. "Father kept her helpless and dependent on him when she was growing up. It was the way young ladies were reared then and she was not too——well, she was never a brainy female. And now she seems——seems muddled, wouldn't you say? So I must be the one, the man in the family, to protect you both."

I wanted to take him in my arms and kiss him, this old man who was so very dear to me. It touched me that he could talk about protecting his sister and me even while he swayed and clutched at me in a spell of vertigo.

"I know that I have been ill!" he said when he had steadied myself. "That is what you're thinking, isn't it, Alicia?" I was afraid that I had wounded his new-found pride in his manhood, but his voice was full of only love when he said, "If there is anything wrong afoot—— and I suspect there is——I must not let it touch my women. You are all I have."

"Dear Grandfather!" I found that I could

139

smile at him. "But you mustn't go wandering about. Now we'll go back and you must soak your feet——"

"Not yet!" He moved away from me although he watched my face closely. "Alicia, who is Cieta?"

The question startled me. I had not been aware that he had even noticed the dark-skinned girl. Whenever she had come into his bedroom, he had seemed to be lost in his own dream world if not actually asleep. I had not known that he had ever heard her name spoken except on the night of our arrival.

"She is——well, she seems to be a servant of some sort. She evidently does the cooking and the housework."

"No, not that, dear child." He shook his head back and forth. "She acts as no servant ever did. I noticed the night we came here, the way she looked when Lottie spoke to her. Yes, tired and worn out as I was, I noticed that. And I wasn't always asleep when she came into my room, although I might have pretended to be. Do you know when she came, how long she has been here? And how has she managed to take over the management of the house from my sister?"

"I do not know, Grandfather."

It was the truth. He was asking questions I had often asked myself and to which I had found no answers.

"What does it matter, at any rate?" I said.

140

"We shall soon be away from this strange place. Grandfather, I have made plans for our leaving. We will take Aunt Charlotte away with us. And Craig. Do you know about the boy whose room is on the fourth floor?"

He said that he did and my amazement heightened. Confined as he had been to his bed, he has missed little of what went on in the house.

"Lottie wrote me something about him in one of her infrequent letters. It was the last one I had from her, I think. I read between the lines of it and detected a note of worry, something about her husband's nephew making no effort to combat whatever it was that kept him in bed. But she never mentioned this woman, Cieta."

"Do not concern yourself with any of it now! Don't let it upset you, Grandfather. We will soon be going. I will arrange to get us away."

"No!" His voice sounded loud and strong in the hush of that dark place. "I must find out what is going on here. I shall not be satisfied until I do."

"But you are not well enough, Grandfather. A man your age!" I had thrown tact to the winds in my concern for him. "We will forget about all this and go back to Boston where I can get proper care for you."

His smile held a faint look of triumph. "Not so old or sick that I did not find out certain things tonight! My coming here to the tower was not in vain. I have discovered what it is that is hidden here. There are people up there!"

I had already guessed that but I did not want to spoil his little moment of gloating. I had not known whether or not the tower was still occupied by anyone other than ourselves and now that my suspicions were confirmed, I glanced nervously up the stairs.

"I do not know how many were there but I heard their voices." Grandfather leaned toward me and began to whisper. "There seemed to be several and I heard some moaning and some praying. What I must know, Alicia, is who these unhappy human beings are and what they are doing up there. I could not climb the stairs and I think I must have fainted. Like a female with the vapors," he finished in self-disgust.

I had heard no sounds from the top of the stairs; perhaps my ears had been deaf in my engrossment with Grandfather. Now what he had told me seemed to conjure them up. They were faint but they were unmistakable. And then there came the soft padding of footsteps coming down the staircase.

My gaze was frozen. I could not have looked away if I had wanted to. The sound of the footsteps became louder and through the near-darkness I saw a face peering down at us. It was as swarthy as Julio's and in it were bright, frightened eyes like bits of shiny glass.

My mouth fell open and I pressed a hand

over it to hold back a scream. Then the face disappeared and I heard the footsteps rushing up and away.

Grandfather was facing in the other direction and so saw nothing except that involuntary movement of my hand to my mouth. And, undoubtedly, the expression on my face.

"You have seen someone? You know now that what I said was true?" he asked softly.

"Yes, yes, I know."

And I wished that I did not. For the certain knowledge that we had of what the tower held would put us both in greater danger, both Grandfather and me. What would happen to us when Cieta learned that we had discovered her secret as, certainly, she must? The answer was horrible, terrifying. I was sure that we would never be allowed to leave Blacktower alive.

CHAPTER ELEVEN

I was young and fairly strong. I had managed to save myself from being smothered by a pillow and I had recovered from the attack in the cemetery. But how could I defend both Grandfather and me in this enclosed place where I knew not how many people were nor what power Cieta had over them to make them do her bidding? The danger was here now, at this minute.

She might even be there at the top of the stairs with the others, listening to what we were saying, taking her time about making a move until she learned how much we knew.

I leaned forward to whisper urgently against Grandfather's ear. "This isn't the time to be taking chances, dear. It is growing light. We must not be seen. We will go back to the house and wait. Later we will see. There will be another time."

There would be no other time. I was deliberately deceiving Grandfather, lying to him because I wanted to get him out of there. And I knew that what I was planning to do must be done at the soonest possible moment. It was too late in the day now. I would have to wait until darkness came again to cover our movements. But how could I protect us both until nightfall? How could I keep us safe?

He was resisting me now, pulling away from me as I tried to lead him out. Frail he might be, but his strong will was still in command.

"I want to stay," he said pettishly, and I could detect, with a sinking heart, the signs of regression into unreality again. His lip thrust out and his face took on that familiar, childish expression.

I spoke quickly in an effort to capture his attention before it began to wander too far away. "Do you know where Ciet? is?"

"I saw her." He seemed to struggle with the memory and I knew that he was not sure whether it was a fresh one or the remembrance of something that had happened long ago. "When I was coming down the staircase, I saw her coming out of the tower door, the one in the hall. But she locked it behind her and put the bar across it. But I knew that there was another door and I went back and found my key and came here."

He looked at me expectantly, waiting for approval, and I patted his shoulder lightly.

"That was very clever of you. Now we will outwit her again, won't we? You must help me, Grandfather. We will go back to the house and we will wait until it is dark. Then tonight all of us—I you and me and Aunt Charlotte and Craig——we will go on another little excursion. You will like that, won't you? It will be

145

like the times you and your sister had secrets from your parents. Only it will be Cieta we will keep the secret from this time."

I repeated that last sentence two or three times more, wanting to impress it on his mind for fear that she might come into his bedroom sometime during the hours that lay ahead. Confused as he was, he might blurt out to her our plans. There was that possibility, although I could not be sure that he would remember, a few hours from now, what I was saying to him at this moment.

At any rate, my words had one good effect. Grandfather did not resist me now. He let me take his arm and lead him to the door. As we came out upon the stone platform, he leaned heavily upon me, all his small supply of strength seeming to be spent. Several times on the way to the house he appeared to be on the point of collapsing and I wondered how I would be able to get him away from it that night—he and poor, bewildered Aunt Charlotte and the boy in the fourth floor bedroom who had not, it seemed, left it in ten years.

I was appalled by the enormity of the task facing me, and yet I knew it must be done. If I remained there, I might be killed. There had been two attacks upon me already; the third one could be more successful. And if I died, the others would be trapped in Blacktower, at the mercy of Cieta until, perhaps, she decided to dispose of them, too.

As we crept in through the side door, I heard sounds of activity in the kitchen, the clatter of dishes and the rushing of water. My heart seemed to freeze into a great, hard lump. I had forgotten about breakfast. Our trays were usually brought up to us long before this. If Cieta had come up to our rooms and found them empty, she would certainly know that something was afoot, if she had not seized upon that knowledge already.

I got Grandfather up the stairs as fast as his exhausted condition would allow. As we went down the hall, he had to stop several times and lean against the wall for a moment or two before he could go on. I was almost carrying him by the time we reached his room.

My fingers racing, I stripped off his coat, removed his shoes and hid them in his closet, and then put him into bed. He fell asleep almost immediately, even before I had returned from my own room where I had gone to throw off my cloak and change my boots.

I had scarcely reached his bedside again when a knock came upon his door. It was Julio bringing the breakfast trays, and I breathed a prayer of thankfulness that it was not Cieta whom I had to face at that moment. Julio sidled into the room in his usual hangdog manner. He did not look up until I spoke his name, and then his eyes merely darted at me from under his lids and slithered away again. His face was closed and sullen and nothing in it encouraged me to go on with what I had been about to say.

But something that morning, perhaps my need for his help, made me see beyond that ruined skin and ugly, scrawny body. I guessed that his disagreeable manner hid a vacuum of loneliness, for he was far away from his homeland——whatever and wherever it might be. He seemed to be a virtual slave of a woman he hated, a stranger in an alien place where people spoke an unfamiliar language and the winters were long and cold and the weather often bleak. I was almost sure that he had come from a warm climate where life had been easier and happier for him. Why had he left its sunshine to come to this remote, unfriendly place? And what made him stay in it?

I wanted to ask him those things, but every moment was important now; not a single one could be wasted with questions I was sure he would not answer anyway.

What I had planned was that I would let him see the money I intended to give him before I told him of my need for a horse and carriage. And that I wanted him to bring one around to the side of the house that night at exactly twelve o'clock.

Midnight was the hour I had chosen for several reasons. There would be enough dark hours preceding it to give me time to get the

148

others ready. Cieta should be asleep by then, for I doubted if there would be any activity around the house tonight. The visits of the ship I had seen were evidently a week or two apart. I had scanned the timetable the station master had given me and knew that a train went through Seamount on its way to Boston at twelve-thirty. We should be able to reach the depot within a half-hour and not have too much time to linger about waiting.

We had arrived at Blacktower at midnight. And we should be leaving it at that hour a few weeks later. How much had happened since that moment I saw its monstrous gates looming in front of me! How could I have guessed that I would be fleeing from it in this manner, taking with me two people I had never seen at that time?

Julio had put down the trays and was starting toward the door with his shuffling gait. I called him back. "Wait for a moment, please! I want to talk to you."

I ran to my bedroom and took a reticule out of a drawer. All our money, both Grandfather's and mine, was in a clasped purse and I opened that with shaking fingers. But when I counted the bills in it, I saw that I only had fifty dollars.

We had discussed how much we would take with us and had decided upon only that amount. For we had agreed that it would be foolhardy to carry a large sum with us on a journey that would stretch through the dark hours of a night. We had been worried about thieves, I remembered. And I had a hysterical impulse to laugh over our nervousness. How paltry that danger seemed now in the face of the present greater one. Now it seemed that we would not be able to escape from it because I did not have a sufficient amount of money with which to bribe Julio.

Fifty dollars——he would never run the risk I was going to ask him to take for such a sum. My spirits sank and I went back to Grandfather's room feeling the heaviness of depression within me. I handed Julio the single dollar bill I held and he snatched it from me with a little grunt of thanks.

Perhaps it would make him feel well-disposed toward me when I finally was able to make my request of him. It might bring me good value. I was still determined to carry out my plans, in spite of this unexpected setback, even when I remembered that I had scarcely enough money to get us very far out of Seamount. I could not remember how much the train fare had been. Perhaps we would not be able to pay our way all the distance to Boston. But if I appealed to the conductor, promised to send him the remainder of the money later——.

No, I was not worried about the railroad fares, only about finding something with which to bribe Julio. And my mind raced over my few belongings.

I owned very little jewelry. My locket, which contained the pictures of my mother and father, was not even to be considered. A brooch, usually worn at my throat, was of twisted, hair-thin filagree; it was neither bright nor shiny and I knew that it would not appeal to Julio. There was nothing else except a signet ring my parents had given me on my tenth birthday. And my watch. Nothing of value, nothing that even caught the eye with its beauty.

Grandfather was still in heavy sleep as I stood there biting my lip in thought. It had seemed better not to awaken him for breakfast, to arouse him to some remembrance, perhaps, of his experience of the early morning. Too, he would need all his strength for what lay ahead of us in the coming night.

My purpose was stronger than ever now, for I saw how faintly he breathed and noted the wax-like texture of his skin. Where could I get hold of some money? The question kept thumping at my brain.

Surely there must be some money somewhere in the house. In a remote place like this, where there was not a banking establishment nearby, people were apt to keep their riches hidden under mattresses and in steel boxes. I had heard many times about Captain Lawson's great fortune. Some of it, at least, must be secreted somewhere in the house.

There was no stirring of my conscience as I

pondered over the prospect of borrowing anything I could find for my purpose. I thought of it as borrowing, although Grandfather surely was entitled to a share of the Lawson money. But if I did come upon any of it and used it, I would return it to Aunt Charlotte at the first possible moment.

What was she doing this morning? I wondered. Could I possibly coax her to tell me where her father's wealth was hidden? I decided to try, and I went along the hall to her room.

She was sitting by a window and the sound of her humming voice came to me as I crossed the threshold. On her lap was a copy of the *Ladies Home Journal* and in her hand was a blunt-edged scissors. I saw that she was cutting the figures in fashion illustrations out of the magazine and standing them up along the window sill.

Her old eyes sparkled with pleasure as she held one of the paper figures up for me to see. "I always do this on rainy days," she chirped happily. "Mama says that playing paper dolls keeps me out of mischief."

Sunshine poured into the room in slanted bars and there was not a sign of a raindrop beyond the window. I stood looking at her hopelessly. She would not be able to tell me anything now for she was once more the little girl whose ears were too young and tender to hear the mundane word "money". Surely she would not be able to tell me, in her present state, where there was any money hidden.

I knew that I must go searching at random, and the logical place to start, it seemed, was the Captain's study. And it occurred to me that if I did not find any actual cash there, the small pieces of silver and jade and ivory must have an impressive value of their own. Surely there would be something among them that would appeal to Julio, something that would persuade him to let me have the horse and wagon. I felt more optimistic now.

From somewhere downstairs, I heard the slamming of a door. The sound seemed to come from the side of the house and I ran from Aunt Charlotte's room and to the window half-way down the hall. From there I saw Cieta walking in the direction of the stable, and I knew I would have no better chance than this to search through the study.

Its door was closed but it was not locked. I stood on the threshold for a moment and looked in. There was no deserted air about this place; I could almost feel the presence of the man who would have spent much of his time here. That, I think, was due to Aunt Charlotte's faithful care. All the small things glittered or glowed. The furniture was polished and the carpet looked freshly beaten.

The carved models, like the skeletons of ghost ships, were frozen forever in motionlessness on their stands. The one on the fireplace mantle was larger than all the rest. That fact and its place of honor led me to believe that this had been a very special ship. I had noticed it only in passing when I had been here on that other occasion. Now I went to the mantle and looked more closely at it.

It was a four-masted schooner with all its sails unfurled and it had on its prow a miniature figurehead of a woman with a proud face and high breasts. Carved into its bow was the name: "HANNAH B." And so I knew that the original ship, which Captain Lawson must have loved above all the others he had sailed, had been named for his wife, the mother of his children.

Not quite sure of where to start my search, I went back in the direction of the desk. Its smooth mahogany surface was bare except for a ship's clock on a stand and a quill pen and inkstand in a marble holder. The drawers along its sides were all locked, but the narrow one along its length slid open when I pulled at its brass knob. I looked through it and found only a few small objects: stubs of pencils, a block of writing paper, and an intricately-carved meerschaum pipe. And a key ring holding three keys.

I took that out and found that one of the keys opened all the other drawers. But in those I discovered nothing at all, no stacks of money nor gold pieces nor jewels. I felt impatient now that I had let my imagination run away with my good sense. I was as bad as Grandfather and Aunt Charlotte with their talk of hidden treasure.

But of course the money, if there was any, would not be left in plain sight for anyone to come upon. I went to peer into the cabinets and tried one of the keys in several of their locks. It opened them all, but I knew nothing about curios or *objects d'art*. I could not guess if any of them had any real value as collectors' items.

As I was passing one of the bookshelves that stretched up on either side of the fireplace, I hesitated over a row of volumes. I had always been an avid reader, finding in books my own form of escape from loneliness or worry. I could no more have passed that shelf without stopping than a starving man could have passed an outthrust hand with food in it.

Some of the titles and authors were familiar to me: *Great Expectations* and *The Odyssey* and *Tales of a Wayside Inn*. There was even *Little Women!* I remembered that Aunt Charlotte had told me that she and Craig had read books together during the time when she was giving him his lessons. These were the ones probably, for I had seen no other library in the house.

When I leaned closer to examine another row of books, I saw that there was a gap between two of the volumes. Something shone there. The light was caught on a dark surface.

I put my hand in the gap and felt the hardness of steel against my fingers. With a quick motion of my hand, I swept the books aside and pulled out of its hiding place a long black box. I had found what I was looking for.

I carried the box over to the desk and tried to push open its lid. Of course it did not open. Who would hide something away in that fashion without locking it? But there had to be some way of opening it and I remembered the third little key. It was still on the surface of the desk and I fitted it into the small hole at the front of the box and heard a snapping sound. The lid opened with a faint squeak as I lifted it.

My first feeling when I saw the contents of the box was bitter, black disappointment. There was no money. There was nothing except papers and a pan of leather-bound books. For a moment I stood staring down at the little volumes, not caring what they were since they were not what I had hoped to find.

And then——through curiosity again——I opened the first one that came to hand. Its pages had grown yellow and stiff with age. The handwriting on them had faded until it was almost impossible to read it. But my eyesight was good and, with a little effort, I began to make sense out of the crowded, spidery lines.

What I held in my hand was the log of the HANNAH B., records of Captain Lawson's sea voyages throughout the years. I turned the crisp pages gingerly and saw names of far away places: China and Africa and the East Indies and a place called Santagracia which I never had heard of before but which appeared with some frequency in the log.

My eyes swept over the recordings of latitudes and longitudes and the entries of money expended and the receipts of cash received for cargoes. And then my glance became captured by certain words and phrases and I went back and reread them. For gradually I began to be aware of what Captain Lawson carried as cargo during the mid-century years. And my fingers began to curl around the little book for now it felt like some horrible, repulsive thing in my hand. I wanted to throw it far away from me, but I went on reading, fascinated and sickened with revulsion at the same time as I learned the source of my great-grandfather's fortune.

The records were all here, complete and detailed and unmistakable. Some were innocuous enough. They told of journeys to the ports of foreign, exotic countries where he had sold New England products——whale oil for lamps and cotton goods and grain and wheat and other staples——to his markets there. Then, on his return voyages, he had filled his hold with spices and silks and the sort of art objects and curios that surrounded me now in the study. He had had a two-pronged method of becoming rich. There had been money waiting for him at both ends of his trips.

Yet that had not satisfied him. For when I picked up the other book and let my eyes race over its pages, I saw that what I had suspected was true. It was not merely hinted at here in this journal. It was written out in full, the infamous activity he had engaged in laid bare.

Captain Lawson's most frequent voyages had been to Africa and in those years before the war between our northern and southern states, he had brought back human beings——Negro slaves——who were to be shipped to plantations in the South. He had trafficked in human misery, grown richer than he needed to be through the disgraceful fact of slavery. The HANNAH B. had been, among other things, a slave ship.

I read on, appalled, not able to put the journal down. And I came to an even more shocking revelation. I had known about slave ships, known that New England sea captains were guilty of plying that nefarious trade. But I had not known about the smuggling of aliens into our shores.

When the war had ended, Captain Lawson had worried about the loss of his income——he wrote that baldly and bluntly. He had had to find some other means of keeping the gold rolling in. And when he had been approached by a native of an island in the Caribbean Sea who sought illegal passage to the United

States, his nefarious activities had begun. The Island of Santagracia had become his point of operation.

He began to engage in a thriving business. No one, evidently, was refused if he had the money—stolen or saved or obtained by any means of all——to pay his passage. Thieves, murderers, law-breakers with prices on their heads, all were crowded into Captain Lawson's ship and brought to America, to this very coastline, hidden in this very house until they could be sent out of it under the cover of darkness.

The money they paid him was carefully set down beside their names and the amounts were staggering. It was little wonder that he had died a very rich man.

Now everything I had seen and heard and learned came whirling into my brain and formed the complete, horrible picture. That ghost-like ship, or perhaps there had been more than one, signalling with a bell that another evil journey had been completed. The sounds of people climbing the rocks. And the scream of some poor wretch weakened by hunger and the long, arduous voyage, no doubt, whose footsteps had been uncertain and who had plunged down the cliff to his death.

And, of course, the weeping and the moaning from behind the tower wall into which the passengers had been smuggled. Sick from the weeks-long journey in a tossing ship, frightened in that dark, unfamiliar, crowded area at the top of the tower steps, they had cried and prayed through the dark hours before they were set free to find some other haven. No doubt some of them had died there and were buried in the unmarked graves in the cemetery. Just as the one who had fallen to his death that morning had been dumped hastily into the gaping pit.

Cieta. Cieta was the guiding spirit in the smuggling. I knew that now. Not why, but merely that she was. I knew, too, that something must have happened on this last journey. A delay of some sort that must have upset her schedule and thrown the operation into confusion. For I was sure that never before had she carried on her illegal activities when there was even the faintest light.

My questions had been answered, my suspicions confirmed. Now I knew the secret of Blacktower.

But there was something which I never would have guessed. I did not have the slightest hint of until I finished reading the part of the journal that pertained to Captain Lawson's trips to Santagracia and picked up a piece of paper at random.

It was an official document on flimsy paper but with the stamp on its corner of the Island of Santagracia. This was a birth record. It set forth the names of a newly-born child, her mother and her father, in the flowing, pretentious handwriting of some minor clerk, perhaps, who was proud of the fact that he knew how to fill out the form. It was dated twenty-five years before.

The child's name was Anacieta Maria Raphealle Rozine Lawson, and she had been born to Relenzia Dolores Maria Marguerita Lawson (née Magdelina), a housemaid, and Simeon Jonas Lawson, birthplace Gloucester, Massachusetts, ship owner, captain and trader.

It was impossible to believe. Yet here it was in undeniable proof, the record that Cieta was my great-grandfather's daughter, born when he was over seventy years old. His daughter, I realized, in every sense of the word.

CHAPTER TWELVE

I picked up the journal again and riffled through it until, almost on the final pages of it, I found the account of that unlikely marriage set forth with as detailed care as everything else I had read so far. It seemed odd that Captain Lawson had written so frankly of his nefarious activities. When I read the story of how he came to marry an island girl, I thought I knew the answer.

"I could not resist her full-blown beauty, as rich and ripe as a summer fruit. Although I wrestled with the devil within me, I was lost from the first moment. It was on a plantation a few miles inland and I was there at the invitation of its owner. He was to give me passage money for a wench who bore his child, for he wanted to send her away and he was willing to give me a goodly sum. She was to be taken to New York where she had relatives who would shelter her, in return for another large sum, and there she was to deliver her bastard baby.

"Relenzia was her sister and she sought me out to beg me to be kind to the unfortunate child——the wench was not yet fourteen years of age. Thus we were alone that night in a clearing at the edge of a jungle. I scarcely heard what she said to me, for lust possessed me at my first glance at her. I attempted to have my way with her but she resisted me, the lesson of her sister undoubtedly too fresh in her mind. And on the other nights when I made excuses to see her and lingered about her like a love-sick schoolboy, she continued to repulse me.

"I was afired with the want of her and I could not mortify my flesh and so I married her, although I knew that it could never be a true marriage and that I must leave her there among her own people when our brief honeymoon was over. To have brought her to Blacktower, where my beloved Hannah had ruled as mistress, was out of the question. I was loathe to reveal my folly to sweet daughter, Charlotte, who has always worshipped me as though I were a god.

"Relenzia was for tropical nights and a bed of soft grass under the stars and a man's last fires of passion. She could have no part of my life at Blacktower. And so I left her in Santagracia, going back several times to indulge my lust."

Thus had this man, dead now for fifteen years, written about the love affair that had satisfied his aged lust and yet seared his conscience. They were strange factors in the person of one man——a New England conscience, lust, greed, the hallowed memory of his wife, the need for love and respect from his daughter.

The journal, I saw now, had been his method of purging himself.

When I read on further, I found the entry pertaining to his final journey to Santagracia. He was very old then, already beset by the illnesses of body and mind that would mark his last days. But he wrote clearly and concisely of discovering that Relenzia had died leaving behind her the ten-year-old child of their marriage.

Realizing, evidently, that his own death was imminent, Simeon Lawson had tried to atone for his sins before he came to the final judgment. The child, Cieta, had been living in the worst sort of squalor; scarcely more than a waif living on the careless charity of everyone and anyone who would befriend her from time to time. Under the torment of his conscience, he had brought her back to Blacktower with him, not acknowledging her but explaining her to Charlotte as the orphan of one of his crew who had been lost at sea.

"But I fear my dear Charlotte is not deceived. Biddable as she is, there are times when she is more astute than I am wont to believe. I have noticed her looking strangely at Cieta when we are at the table together."

There were no more clear-cut entries. The ones that followed were illegible or meaningless and had been written, undoubtedly, when the Captain's mind first began to deteriorate. And so I had only a teasing hint of what it had been like at Blacktower with the three of them together——Cieta perhaps bewildered at first, Charlotte puzzled, and the old man slipping into senility still not acknowledging his dark-skinned daughter.

Then death had come to him and so the book would have lain untouched for the past fifteen years. . . .

But was that actually so? If I had come upon the steel box with so little trouble and discovered so easily the way to open it, it was only logical to assume that Charlotte, too, had found it and read it at one time or another. Perhaps even before her father's death. That could account for her "looking strangely" at Cieta, as the Captain had noticed and written about. And it would explain why she had allowed her half-sister to assume a place of equal importance, or of even greater authority than her own, in the household.

I stuffed the papers and books back into the box and locked it. Then I carried it to its hiding place on the shelf and replaced the keys in the desk drawer. I moved swiftly for I was impatient now to talk to Aunt Charlotte; to try to find out from her, if I could, why she had allowed Cieta to carry on the same sort of illegal activities their father had engaged in before his death.

It was doubtful, of course, if she could tell me anything in her fuzzy-brained state. But I had to try. And so I sped up the stairs and through the door of her bedroom.

She was still sitting by the window, but her hands were idle and her eyes were dreaming. I went to her and knelt down beside her and gathered her in my arms. She looked so defenseless and vulnerable that I struggled with my disinclination to use the cruel means I knew were necessary if I were to shock her into understanding what I must say to her.

"Aunt Charlotte!"

I waited until she looked at me before I spoke again. "Cieta is your half-sister, isn't she?"

Bright color swept up from her throat and once more her skin looked like the covering of a dried apple. Her tiny mouth began to tremble and for a moment I feared that she would burst into tears. But her eyes remained dry and there was a brightness in them that told me that my words had not only penetrated her poor addled brain but had shocked her with a shattering force.

She cried, "How did you know?"

"I saw the papers. And the log and the journal. You read them, too, didn't you, Aunt Charlotte?"

"A long time ago." She drew a long, ragged breath. "It was when he first brought her here. I didn't know who she really was, nor did she suspect, I think, at the time either. But I suspected right from the start. For I was sure

Father had no——no foreigners among his crew."

She broke off and sat torturing her fingers, each hand busy with the other. For a long time she did not speak and I began to be afraid that she would tell me nothing more. She lay limp in my arms and I rocked her gently back and forth as though she were a child in need of comfort, but she did not seem to notice the movement of our bodies together. Finally she drew away from me and I saw that her face was puckered with anxiety.

"You will not tell anyone——ever? All these years I have kept the secret, for I could not bear to have anything tarnish the name of my father. Can you not imagine how people would have laughed if it were known that he had married a young girl when he was seventy years old? He was strong and handsome even then, but he had the ships and much money and I believe that it was the money——that he bought that woman's love. But why did he want her? He had me to love him and care for him."

Poor Aunt Charlotte! She had read the journal and yet not read it. Her eyes had seen certain words and phrases but she had not let her brain accept them. She had refused to believe that her father had been a lecherous old man and gone on burying his clay feet in her idolatry.

"It was not his fault," she murmured. "But to

have become a father at that age! People would have considered him a——a freak, a monster. I loved him dearly, Alicia dear. I could not let him be laughed at or censured even after he died."

Here was more proof of her slavish devotion, but I still could not believe that it would go to such lengths that she would allow Cieta to carry on her criminal activities without interference. And surely Aunt Charlotte must know what was going on. She could not have been so blind and deaf that she remained unaware of how the tower was being used. We would come to that subject later. There was something I wanted to get clear in my mind first.

"And what of Cieta? She must have learned the truth of her parentage. She would not be so arrogant, so high-handed unless she knew."

"She found the books and the papers, too. I remember the very day that must have happened. She came into this room here and told me that she was taking no more orders——she could not have been more than sixteen at the time but she seemed suddenly to have grown into a woman. What she said, too, was that she intended to give some orders of her own. Yes, she learned everything, of that I am sure. I think she must have found in that box the names of the men who had made up Father's crews, no doubt that of his first mate and learned where she could reach him and so got

168

in touch with him. For how else would she get the ships——?"

Aunt Charlotte broke off suddenly and a hand flew to her lips.

I said, "Do not be concerned. You haven't revealed anything I didn't know before. Of course I heard the things that were going on, actually saw one of the people she smuggled in. You knew about all this and yet you never went to the authorities?" My voice had grown a little stern. "You let her go on breaking the law and said nothing to anyone about it?"

She looked at me with shimmering eyes and her mouth was tremulous again. "What could I do? Oh, Alicia, what was I to do? To have told would have brought out the story of what my father had done. And the——the rest. The Lawson name would have been disgraced forever. Exposure of the smuggling would bring even greater shame to it than that sinful marriage."

For some reason I thought of Craig. "Does Craig know, too?" I demanded. "He must, of course. Then why has he never tried to communicate with anyone? He could have found some way of getting a letter out of the house, surely. Aunt Charlotte, you must tell me! Is he in love with Cieta?"

She averted her glance. "Craig is——is sick. I am not sure what is between them. When he came, ten years ago, he was twelve and Cieta was fifteen. They were the only young people

169

in the house and they had no contact with anyone else except me. As he grew into young manhood, he had no other companion except Cieta. She insisted on caring for him, stopped his lessons and refused to let me near him. I know that she loves him. And he——well, he is completely dependent upon her."

Again I could detect evasiveness in her manner. But I did not have the heart to press her further. The subject of Craig seem to agitate her and now her head was moving from side to side like that of a trapped animal.

So I said only, "I do not believe that Craig is as sick as Cieta tries to make him think he is. Aunt Charlotte, we must get him away from here. All of us will go——you and I and Craig and Grandfather."

Her eyes widened and she shrank away from me. "But that is impossible!"

"Not if you will help me. Don't you understand? Grandfather and I have discovered her secret and she will not hesitate to kill us both——I am sure of that. It is different with you. She knows you could not expose her. But we have no reason for keeping silent. Grandfather has never had the sort of feelings you have for your father. And she would do anything to seal our lips. Oh, Aunt Charlotte," I begged, "listen to me! Grandfather is old and sick and he needs help. Please, please! We can go away this very night if I can only lay my hands on enough money to pay Julio to let us have the horse and wagon."

A sudden inspiration made me ask, "Do you have any money anywhere around?"

She got up stiffly and moved, like someone dream-walking, toward her dresser. It was as though I had imposed my will upon her by my urgency, for her hands seemed to move mechanically as she opened the drawer and rummaged around in it. When she came back to me she was carrying a teakwood box. She waited for me to open it and I did. It was stuffed with old bills and gold pieces.

Now that her errand was completed, all Aunt Charlotte's strength seemed to leave her and she sank back down into the chair like someone whose bones had collapsed. I knew that I must not waste time, for unless I gave her instructions quickly, her mind would be too far away to grasp what I was saying.

I told her that she must go to bed that night with all her clothes on and pull the coverlet up to her chin so that if Cieta happened to look in she would not know that Aunt Charlotte was fully dressed. I repeated three times that I would return at midnight and that it would be better if she remained awake so that I would not have to take the time to arouse her. As I said all those things, she nodded and murmured and I was sure that she understood me.

With the money in my hand, I was ready to approach Julio. I left Aunt Charlotte still murmuring and went to crouch by the head of the staircase. In a little while I heard Cieta come in through the side door and listened to her footsteps recede in the direction of the kitchen. When a door slammed in that part of the house, I slipped quietly down to the first floor and ran out to the stable.

Julio was rubbing down the horse's legs, his scrawny body bent in an awkward position. He did not see me at first but then he looked up and his ravaged face seemed to grow even darker.

"I have told you eet ees bad for you to come. Today——now——thees ees worse time of all——"

I thrust out my hand. I let him see the bills and the gold pieces and, as I had been sure they would, his small eyes gleamed with yearning.

"It is all for you, Julio," I told him. "I will give it to you if you will help me tonight. I want to have the wagon hitched and ready beside the house at midnight. We are going away, my grandfather and I, and we must do it without being seen. I cannot take the time now to tell you why, but we have to go. Look, Julio! You will be rich. There is a great deal of money here. Will you do what I ask?"

Stark terror seemed to have overcome him while I was speaking. His jaw trembled and his nose twitched spasmodically. Little gurgling noises sounded in his throat. And then he began to gulp and finally words poured out of his shaking mouth.

"No! No! I cannot do it. She would keel me! Tonight——you want me to do thees tonight? But thees ees when she would have me take the others away. Eet ees why she come just now——to tell me. I am to take them in the wagon, like always. I am busy now to get the beast ready."

I stared back at him in mute, despairing silence, appalled by my own stupidity. Why had I not realized before that of course the people in the tower would be allowed to stay there only until the first possible moment they could be sent away? Cieta would shelter them for only a single night and then she would turn them out. Julio was her ally, this was his function at Blacktower. And I had chosen for our flight the very same time the people who had been smuggled into the tower would be leaving it.

"Where do they go? Where do you take them?"

It could not matter to me now, but I asked the question anyway. Julio spoke promptly, his eyes still on the money. "Eef I tell you, you weel pay me?"

I handed him one of the gold pieces and his fingers closed over it swiftly.

"There ees a place, ten miles from where are the houses and the store."

"From the village you mean?"

"Si, the veelage. Where I go, eet ees what you call a crossroads. I leave them there and then they go to the north country——you call eet Canada? If they lucky they can get across the border. If they have money, they can find someone to help them. But the ones who have not enough money when she ees finished with them——" His narrow shoulders lifted in a shrug. "The way ees long. They die in the cold sometimes. She have turned out some who do not have enough to pay her for me to take them to the crossroads. I do not know what happen to them. Sometimes, I theenk, she have to keel the ones who are so seeck when they get here they can go no further. For she afraid they die on the road and be found. She take no chances, Cieta."

The pictures I saw in my imagination were so horrible that I was trembling as violently as Julio was by the time he finished talking. I could see those huddled, frightened figures in the wagon; being turned out of it on a cold, unfamiliar road; plodding ahead, if they were still lucky enough to be alive by that time, to the border station where arrest and ultimate return to their own country might await them. Cieta stripped them of their money and gave them only hardship or death, imprisonment or exile.

I had known the evil of her activities but not the extent of that evil. And for a moment or two I could simply stare mutely at Julio while the sickness of revulsion churned inside me.

Finally I asked, "At what time will they be going? When does she plan to have you take them away?"

I had to give him another gold piece before he would answer that. "At the hour of two. She have geeven me a clock. I can tell the hours," he added proudly. "Always when eet ees two o'clock at the other times, I am ready."

"We could be gone by then. You could take us to the station and be back here before two."

He shook his head. She would know, he said. Cieta——and here his fear almost seemed to get out of control——had strange powers. She would know what he had done. "She weel keel me," he said again.

"This is why you stay on here? Because you are afraid of her 'strange powers'? Julio, that is nonsense. Why don't you go away?" My voice began to hoarsen with urgency. "You could escape, too. I will give you this money. You could take the train with us and when we get to Boston, I will see that you get a good job. I have many friends there and I'm sure one of them would take you on as a coachman. Have you ever been to Boston, Julio? It is not like here where there is nothing to see or do. There are theatres, stores; many people, many horses and carriages. You would like it, I know."

Now that I had seized upon that way of achieving my own ends, my words were tum-

175

bling over each other in my eagerness. I watched his face closely as I spoke and I saw the wistful look that spread over it.

"Please!" I went on frantically. "You would be a rich man. You would not have to live in a stable with only a horse for company. Do you like music, dancing? Perhaps you would meet a girl there, for people of all nationalities land at Boston——it is a busy port. You would like to get married, wouldn't you? Here in this place you are nothing more than a prisoner."

I could not be sure that he understood all that I was saying but his yearning expression told me that some of my words, at least, had had an effect. Then he drew a long sigh and shook his head.

"She needs me. Even eef I go she would know where I am. She would breeng me back."

"Julio, she could not bring you back against your will! We could go to the police——"

"Poleeza!" He cowered back in sudden panic and I knew that I had said the wrong thing. I had guessed by then that Julio was one of the poor wretches Cieta had brought into the country illegally, that he undoubtedly had been a law-breaker in his homeland or, perhaps, an escaped criminal. This was the whip she had held over him, the thread that kept him in her thrall.

"You are afraid of the police, Julio?"

The word made him wince again and he seemed unable to answer me so I went on

176

speaking. "Cieta has told you that you will be arrested and sent back to your own country if you leave this place?"

His head hung forward as he nodded. He looked beaten and helpless and I wanted to reassure him.

"But she could not do that, don't you see?" I spoke carefully so that he would understand what I was saying. "If she told the authorities about you, she would be confessing her own crimes. She has only said that——threatened you with arrest——to keep you here to do her bidding. Because she needs you to get the people away. Julio, why don't you come with us? You will be free in the city."

The knowledge smote me that, in effect, I would be abetting a crime myself in not reporting his presence to the police. But I did not know what his offense had been in that faraway island. I had heard that people were thrown into jail for petty reasons or political ones; and surely by this time Julio had paid for his crime with his virtual imprisonment here at Blacktower all these years. The end, I told myself, justified the means. For by getting all of us away, I might be preventing some more horrible crime.

Then another thought struck me. Someone had attacked me in the cemetery. What I might be doing was asking a potential murderer to come along with us.

"Julio," I said, staring right into his eyes.

177

"Did you hit me this morning right after I came to you to ask you to help me find my grandfather? Someone did. Someone struck me and left me there unconscious."

"I deed not do eet. I swear eet! By the Holy Mother I swear eet was not me."

I believed him. He went on fingering the medal that hung on a chain around his throat. The shiftiness was gone from his eyes and he had spoken in a loud, clear voice. Then he looked down again at the money in my hand.

Finally he said, "You theenk eet weel be safe? Then yes, I weel go weeth you. For I want no more of the keelings, the deaths. The horse and wagon, I weel have them hidden in the side yard. There ees a place where there ees grass and around eet the trees are theeck and here the beast and the cart weel not be seen. Eet must be just when you say——at twelve o'clock. For eef we do not get away queeck——"

Relief flooded over me and, for a moment, left me weak and dizzy.

CHAPTER THIRTEEN

Now there remained only Craig to be told. I had left him for the last; had I waited too long to prepare him for what was ahead?

The afternoon was coming to a close. The hours had fled while I had lingered over Captain Lawson's papers and talked to Aunt Charlotte and Julio.

As I ran back to the house, I thought I felt eyes upon me once more. But I did not look up at Craig's window this time. Perhaps he would be puzzled, if he were watching me there, by my haste and disheveled appearance. But it could not matter now. Soon I would be telling him everything, explaining it all to him.

I very nearly came face to face with Cieta. She was in the front hall locking the inside tower door. She had an empty water pitcher dangling from one hand and she turned just as I came in through the side door. What she had been doing, I supposed, was catering to the needs of the poor wretches who were soon to be turned out; she would not want another death so soon after the other one. Time would be precious for her, too. The digging of a new grave and the burial of another body would upset her plans by the delay.

Fear put a constricting lump in my throat so that I could scarcely breathe as I stood there only a few feet away from her. But she had not heard me nor looked in my direction before I shrank back from the door. She dropped the iron bar over the latch and it made a loud, clanging noise in the stillness.

A few minutes later I heard her footsteps dying away and then the slamming of the kitchen door.

I drew a long, deep breath in preparation for my journey over the staircase, and I tried to walk up slowly in order to reserve my strength, because the night would be a long one. But even so, I was breathless when I reached Craig's room.

I stood for a moment looking in on him. His eyes were shut but he did not appear to be sleeping heavily. When I went to his bed, I saw that lying beside it were a pair of brightly-polished shoes. The sight of them touched me as nothing else could have done. Poor Craig! my heart cried. He was allowed to walk as far as the window, never to leave his room. Yet he had blackened his shoes as carefully as though he were a young dandy with a crowded social calendar.

I spoke to him softly, "Craig!"

In that instant while his eyelids were fluttering, I wondered what sort of mood I would find him in today. For I had seen him sweet and amiable, restless and unfriendly. Would he be grateful of the chance to escape or reject my plans for him? Did he want to be free or was he satisfied to remain Cieta's prisoner forever? What, actually, did I know about anything he might feel or want?

Then I looked down at the shoes again and they settled the matter for me. Why would they be there, unless their owner sometimes dreamed that he would put them on and walk away on them?

I was more than ever determined now to help him. He looked very young and boyish as he lay there, a lock of fair hair tumbling over his forehead and his eyelashes silken against the pallor of his skin. I would always remember him as he looked now; in future days the picture of him would haunt me, I knew, if I went away and left him to Cieta.

His eyes were open now and he was completely alert, not having to struggle or shake off sleep as most people do upon awakening.

I went closer to him. "Craig, there is something I have to tell you. But first you must answer a question. Are you really very ill? Could you——could you take a journey?"

His blue eyes stared into mine blankly. "A journey? Where to?"

I told him then that we were going away that night, Grandfather and I and Aunt Charlotte and Julio.

"There is evil in this place. Surely you must know that, too. You could not have been unaware of what is going on. Now that Grandfather and I have discovered the truth, we are in danger. The others also——when Cieta finds out they helped us——will not be safe here. She—— you must answer me this time. You do not love Cieta, do you?"

He seemed to consider that for a moment or two and then he said, "She is my friend."

"She is nobody's friend. For years she has forced Aunt Charlotte to keep the secret of the dreadful things she is doing. Julio is her slave, kept here under the threat of turning him over to the authorities."

I told him everything I had discovered and finished by describing the arrangements I had made for getting us all out of there that night.

"Will you come, too, Craig?"

He went deeper into thought and his eyes began to grow brilliant with a glitter of excitement. When he continued to hesitate over his answer, I said, "If you are worrying about your illness, there are fine hospitals and doctors in Boston. I do not know what is wrong with you. Aunt Charlotte wouldn't or couldn't tell me, but surely it is something that can be cured. I think it is tragic that you have been confined here so long! I know that you have had no schooling since you arrived, except for the lessons Aunt Charlotte gave you. Yet you have a quick wit and an intelligent mind. Your books have served you well. But you should have formal training. Wouldn't you like to enroll as a pupil in a real school, perhaps go on to college?"

I was tempting him, as I had tempted Julio, but with a different kind of bait. And again I was successful. He motioned his head up and down.

"When will you do this, Alicia? When do you plan to leave?"

"At midnight. Exactly on the dot of twelve. You must be there in the clearing a little way beyond the house at exactly that time. I will have to manage to get Grandfather and Aunt Charlotte downstairs and out of the house so I will not be able to help you. You will have to do it alone. Do not bring any luggage, nothing that will be heavy or cumbersome, because suitcases will only be in the way. And the wagon will be crowded enough with the five of us in it. Whatever you need we can purchase in Boston. You can manage to get down and out to the side yard, can't you?"

He nodded again, his face alive as the excitement seemed to spill out of his eyes and spread over all his body. His hands were twiching, when I left him, as though he could not contain his eagerness and impatience.

I was impatient and nervous myself as I waited for the hours to pass. Julio brought us our supper trays, keeping his face averted and hurrying in and out of the room. After that there was nothing to do except sit quietly and count the passing hours.

Grandfather was in his arm chair where I had put him so that he would not fall into a sleep so deep it would be difficult to arouse him from it. He sat there fully dressed, his head nodding as he dozed. Once it grew heavy and plunged forward so that he almost toppled from the chair and he awoke and stared at me in bewilderment. He could not comprehend, I knew, why I was keeping him from his bed and why the lamp was still burning low on the table beside him.

For the twentieth time that night I leaned forward to the light and looked at my watch which hung from a fleur-de-lis pin on my shirtwaist. Not satisfied with the slow passage of time, I compared it with Grandfather's heavy gold timepiece which he kept in his pocket. He had owned it since his twenty-first birthday and it had not been more than a minute or so innaccurate in all these years.

And finally the slowly-moving hands pointed to fifteen minutes before the hour of twelve. It was time for us to get ready to go.

"Grandfather!" I shook his shoulder lightly. "We must start now. The wagon will be waiting for us and we don't want to be late."

I could see his eyes shining in the dim light. They were as empty as a baby's and I knew that he did not remember a single thing that had happened early that morning nor anything that I had said to him about going away.

So great was my exasperation that I had to bite my lips to keep from crying out at him. I knew that I must keep my nerves and temper under control. And it was not his fault, of

184

course, that his brain had become blurred again. Now I must find some way of getting through those layers of fuzziness to reach him.

"We are going away. Remember I told you? Remember how I said that you and I and Charlotte would be taking a little trip, something like the excursions you and she used to go on when you were children? It was fun, wasn't it?" I coaxed. "And you were kind to take her with you. For she couldn't have gone unless you took care of her and made sure that she didn't fall or hurt herself in any way. Poor Charlotte! She is rather helpless, you know. She wouldn't be able to go tonight if you weren't there to watch over her."

My words seemed to have torn through the clouds in his mind. He asked in a concerned voice, "Lottie will be out tonight? But she never left the house after dark. You are quite right. She does need me with her," and he struggled out of the chair and then stood quietly while I put his heavy coat on him and pulled a woolen cap down over his ears.

My cloak was waiting on a chair nearby. I threw it over my shoulders, turned down the lamp and opened the door. Grandfather seemed to need no help as we went down the hall through the red haze of the gas globe.

When we stopped in front of Aunt Charlotte's room, I stood still and listened for a moment or two. I could detect no sounds from anywhere else in the house, but from behind the door came the unmistakable heavy breath-

ing and whistling noise of snoring. The feeling
of exasperation rose in me again. Was nothing
to go right?

There were no lights in the bedroom and
Aunt Charlotte's figure was only a dark mound
under the coverlet. I hoped against hope that
she had followed my orders about not undress-
ing, but when I went to her and touched her, I
felt the long, flowing sleeve of her nightgown.

"Aunt Charlotte," I hissed. "You must get up!
You didn't do what I told you, did you? You
shouldn't have——"

Her head lolled in my direction and I had to
shake her before she came awake. And I had to
light her lamp because I did not know where
her clothes were. And then when I had found
them and had her on her feet, Grandfather had
to stand waiting in the hall because he could
not remain in the room while his sister was
dressing. That, in itself, represented danger.

Every minute counted. Her not having followed my instructions could mean the ruina-
tion of my plans. Already, I knew, we were
running behind the schedule I had set for us. I
got her into her corset and corset cover and
underdrawers and petticoats and dress. Her
coat was long and bulky and one of her arms
became stuck in a sleeve.

She hung back as I was urging her toward
the door. She realized, through what means I
do not know, that her hair hung in dangling
braids over her shoulders; and she wanted to
unplait it and arrange it properly. In that mo-

ment of unexplained clarity, she even mumbled about clean white gloves!

I refused to allow her to delay us further. We would be a strange-looking group to be boarding a late train to the city. But it did not matter. I wanted us out of there, to get down to the side yard before Julio despaired of our coming or became frightened by the fact that we were not on time.

A thick blanket of night fog pressed against the front entrance, swirled around our heads as I half-led, half-pushed the two on either side of me down the steps toward the lane that led up to them. I was not quite sure where the clearing was, but finally we came upon it. I saw the outlines of the horse and wagon through the mist and my relief was so great that it almost turned to hysteria. I wanted to shout now, not from anger or frustration, but because of the success of my plans.

There was someone waiting in the shrubbery beside the house and he began to follow us. The whispering, uneven footsteps came closer and closer. I whirled and saw him, that small figure at our heels, and my first thought was that it was Julio who had been hiding there until our arrival.

But it was not Julio; he was much shorter of stature than Julio or me or even Grandfather and Aunt Charlotte, short as they were. He did not come even to my shoulder. The light of the wagon lamp fell on his face and I turned away. I could not bear to look at Craig then.

His limp was a pronounced one, the lifting of one foot high off the ground and the other pulled along behind it. It was his tiny legs, cruelly twisted, that diminished his height. From the waist up he was perfectly formed, his head well set on broad shoulders, but the rest of his body had been all but destroyed.

As I turned away after that brief glance at him, I remembered what Aunt Charlotte had told me about the accident which had killed his father and mother. "Craig was riding with them." And I had assumed that he had escaped injury. But he had not. And it had been an ugly sort of maiming, this crippling of a young boy of twelve.

I knew now, in a wash of pity, why Craig spent all his time in bed. He would be unable to do the things other boys did——run and jump and swim and play ball. Even walking was difficult for him. I realized how much effort coming this far had meant.

I moved away from the others and put out my hand to him, trying to say in the pressure of my fingers on his arm all the things I could not say in words. I asked an innocuous question. "You have been waiting long?"

"Yes. In the shadows of the house until I saw you come out. I——I——It took me a while to get downstairs."

"Of course." I made my voice sound matter-of-fact. "But you are here and that's the important thing. Come, we mustn't waste time. Julio will help you into the cart."

But Julio was standing beside the horse like something carved in wood and his eyes, riveted on Craig's face, had stark fear in them. Even in the misty light I could see that shine of terror in them and something of his feeling, although I did not understand it, communicated itself to me. I was trembling with impatience to be away, away and out of the shadow of Blacktower behind us.

I cried, "Julio, we haven't got all night! Will you please help the others into the wagon? I can get in myself but——"

It was plain that he didn't hear me. He could not seem to tear his gaze away from Craig. He cried out so loudly that the sound of his voice made me wince with fear that he would be overheard. "Not heem! I do not take heem!"

I could not imagine why this whim had suddenly come upon him. "Julio, I don't know what's got into you." I began to speak rapidly, almost incoherently. "We made a bargain today, didn't we? I told you I'd give you the money and that you could come away with us. Look, I have it right here in my hand!"

I held it out for him to see, but this time the magic did not work. He didn't even look at the bills and gold pieces. He cowered back against the horse's flank and his body seemed to have shrunk into his clothing.

"Why you do eet I do not know." His voice made a gurgling sound. "But heem! She weel keel us all! For Meester Craig to go——I do not understand. No, no! Thees I cannot do!"

"Then stay!" I cried out in disgust. I turned to Craig. "Do you know how to drive?"

He nodded. "A long time ago. My father taught me. It is not something you forget, I think."

"Then we will take the wagon. Julio, I will give you the money if you will let us have it. We can leave it at the depot and you can find some way of getting it back. I don't care how you explain it to Cieta. You can say we stole it, took it without your knowledge. With the money you can find a way to get out of here yourself."

He seemed too frozen to make any reply nor any demur when I forced the money into his hand. His eyes were still on Craig and I thought, "He knows how Cieta feels about Craig. He is afraid of what she would do when she discovers he is gone." But there was no point in lingering on that. Julio was not going but he did nothing to prevent Craig from taking the reins from his hands.

At that moment something came bounding out of the bushes with loud, joyous yelps. The great hairy dog whom I had befriended and whom I had named "Prince" threw himself at me in ecstasy at our reunion.

Julio hissed, his voice almost lost in the barking, "Make heem be quiet! He weel have them all awake with his noise. Then eet weel be bad."

190

He stooped and picked up a piece of tree branch and brandished it at the dog's head. If I had not caught his arm he would have struck Prince.

"You could kill him with that! It is not his fault. He remembers me and he's glad to see me. I'll take care of him."

But I was overly-optimistic. The sound of barking went on and on, filling the air around us and seeming to echo above the dim thunder of the waves beyond the house.

"Prince!" I begged while the powerful body lunged at me, fell back and then leaped on me again.

Finally he grew quiet and rolled over at my feet. As I was helping Aunt Charlotte into the back seat of the wagon, he pushed past her and jumped up over its wheel. He found himself a place to sit and settled into it. I knew that he did not intend to let us go away without him.

No one, myself included, seemed to feel inclined to drag him out of the wagon. My nerves were beginning to feel like tightly-strung wires that would snap at any moment. Craig put up a hand but I said, "Let him stay there. When we get to the village he will find his way to wherever he lives. He must have strayed away from one of the farms and no doubt will come upon it eventually."

Grandfather and Aunt Charlotte had drawn close together again and stood like two huddled, frightened children. I took them by turn and

and pushed them into the back of the wagon. They did nothing to help themselves and they felt like dead weights in my arms.

I did not look while Craig was climbing into the driver's box. How he managed it I do not know; I could not bear to witness that painful ascent. When I did look up, he was settled there with the reins in his hands and I got in beside him.

He spoke softly to the horse and slapped the reins against her rump. We were away at last.

The clopping of hoofs and the creaking of the wagon sounded loud in the stillness of the night. We went sweeping past Julio and I wondered if he would return to the stable, set out on his own flight or go back to Blacktower to betray us to Cieta. I did not turn my head because I couldn't have remained even reasonably calm in that last eventuality.

It did not seem possible that Cieta could have slept through all the noise of the barking and our voices. And I expected that momentarily she would come after us, managing, in some way, to overtake us.

There were no sounds behind us but I did not breathe easily until I saw the monstrous gates looming in front of us. My relief was short-lived. For suddenly I realized that I did not know how to open them and that Grandfather, who seemed not to have breathed nor moved since I had put him into the wagon, might not remember now the trick of unlatching the lock.

CHAPTER FOURTEEN

I seized Craig's arm and cried, "The gates!" He turned his face in my direction. It was rigid and his jaw was clamped. I could see the excited glitter of his eyes.

"Do you know how to open them? Surely you must!"

"Not me. I haven't been through them in ten years. You mean you don't know, either?"

"Grandfather did it the night we came. And I didn't notice how." My voice was growing shrill. "They must be locked."

Craig said, "If he did it once, he should be able to again."

"But that was before he——he——" I turned around and looked at that motionless figure in the back seat. He looked like something in a wax museum, his face shining palely in the fog, his hands lying over each other in his lap. "Grandfather?"

He did not answer me, and I knew that he had closed himself off from what was happening around him by retreating into some far-away place in his mind.

Craig pulled on the reins and the horse's gait became slower and then the wagon came to a stop. I could not bear the thought that the gates would spell our defeat, that we must turn around and go back to Blacktower to slink into it like criminals to face the consequences of our wrong-doing. The picture of what would await us there made me jump from the wagon and run around to the back of it.

There was no one to help me get Grandfather out of it. I could not ask Craig to make that labored climb again. My breath came raggedly from the physical effort and from the pumping of my heart in fright.

Grandfather was limp, an over-ized rag doll in my arms. And when I finally got him to the ground and propelled him to the gates, he merely stood there with his head hanging down, not seeming to know where he was and with no sign that he understood what I was begging him to do.

Minutes were passing. I made one last effort. "Grandfather," I cried, "you must open them for us! You know how to do it. Please try to remember!" and then gave up in hoplessness and despair. I knew that it was no use.

While I stood there, blinded by my tears, Aunt Charlotte's voice came sailing out to me from where she was sitting. It sounded high and petulant.

"Why don't you do what she wants you to, Jasper? You're just being stubborn, you naughty boy! You know all you have to do is press down on the lever and slide up the bolt. Honestly, Jasper, sometimes I don't blame Father a bit

194

for being angry with you! You can be so exasperating!"

I gave her a look full of love and gratitude. Then I groped for the lever, found it and pressed hard on it. Something made a clicking sound and the bolt slipped upward. The gates creaked as I threw my weight upon them. They swung open and I pushed until the space between them was wide enough for the horse and wagon to go through.

Grandfather let me help him back to his place. By the time I was beside Craig again, every nerve in my body seemed to be trembling. But ahead was the road leading to the village and it led to freedom. When the wagon made the turn and we were at last on our way, I began to feel light-headed, almost giddy.

Then from somewhere far off I heard, through the noise of the horse and wagon, the mournful wail of a train whistle. Now consternation was back upon me again. I unpinned my watch from my shirtwaist and leaned forward to read it in the swaying light of the wagon.

My worst fears were a fact. The tiny hands pointed to almost twelve-thirty. We were too late. All the delays——having to dress Aunt Charlotte, Prince's playfulness, Julio's defection at the last minute, the long while it had taken to get the two old people into the cart, the moments we had spent at the gate——had eaten up time and ruined my schedule.

Craig heard my whimper of frustration. "What is it?"

I told him that we would be too late for the train which even now must be nearing the Seamount depot. "I don't know what we will do now. I thought only of getting on that train. I didn't plan any alternative. Now——well, it is out of the question for us to stand around the station all night waiting for the morning train. Grandfather and Aunt Charlotte are close to exhaustion now.

"There must be someone I can go to, someone who would help us. Why of course there is!" and the words burst from my lips as my purpose suddenly crystallized.

Several times during the long day just past, I had thought, in passing, of the police. I knew that sometime in the future——a vague time which was nowhere near definite in my mind ——I would have to inform the authorities what I had discovered at Blacktower, what Cieta had done and was doing and about the multiple deaths she had caused.

All along, ever since I had discovered her secret and heard from Julio how she disposed of the people she had smuggled in, I had known that I must do this eventually. For one thing there was the Lawson money which belonged, in part, to Grandfather and Aunt Charlotte and which they would need in their old age. I could not let them relinquish all claim to it. And I knew that I would not be able to go on living with the eyes of my conscience shut while Cieta went on trafficking in human misery.

Now, out of need for shelter for all of us, I came to the point of action.

"There must be a sheriff in the village," I said to Craig. "Somehow we can manage to find him. Perhaps I shall have to ring doorbells, rouse sleeping people out of their beds. But I must secure protection for us for tonight, a place where you three will be safe. And where you can rest and get warm."

"You are going to the authorities and tell them about Cieta?"

"Of course!" I turned to look at him in surprise. "She cannot go unpunished. Not after what she has done to you and Aunt Charlotte and Julio, what she is doing this very night to those poor souls in the tower. Now after she has smuggled them in and taken what money they had, she will turn them out to die."

He said softly, "You are very brave, Alicia. And very clever. How did you learn so much about all this in the first place? You did not tell me that."

"I thought I had. It was the tower and the feeling of evil about the house. I heard the voices of those poor people and the sounds from outside. When I found Captain Lawson's journal and saw someone today——"

My voice began to peter out and my head turned in his direction. I saw the reins slack in his hands. The horse had slowed down to a jogging pace as I had been speaking. Now she was scarcely moving.

I asked, "Craig, what is it? Even though we've missed the train, there is no time to lose. The two back there are apt to become chilled. I don't want them catching cold."

We were on a dark stretch of road where the walls of trees on either side of us were the thickest. The lantern threw only scanty light, but the mists had lifted as the distance between us and the ocean had lengthened. Ahead I could see the curve that shut off the road beyond at this point.

A puzzled uneasiness began to spread over me. I turned to look at Craig. His eyes were bright with a wild light and his mouth stretched over his teeth in a strange grimace that had no resemblance to a smile.

I said faintly, "Craig! Why are we stopping here? What is the matter? Are you ill?"

He did not answer me. He put his hand into his pocket and when he took it out again, something caught the light and gleamed. Horror, cold and leaping, washed over me as I realized that it was a long, thin blade.

He motioned it in my direction and said in a voice that sounded gleeful, "You did not really think I would let you get away, did you? Come on, get out of here!"

I shrank away from him until I was at the edge of the seat, and I had no choice but to obey him. He followed me with the knife held pointing at my throat.

"Oh, Craig!" I whispered. "Why? Why?"

But I did not have to ask. I knew. I could see it in my mind, hear it all as though I had actually been there while he was telling her.

——*"They are going away, all of them. She asked me to go with them and I said I would, so that I could learn her plans. That was the right thing to do, wasn't it, Cieta?"*

——*"You were clever, Craig dear. And you must play along with the scheme, pretend that you are going with them. Then, when you have them all together, when you are in some remote spot where it is dark, you know what you must do. For we cannot have her running to the police to tell them what she knows. The old man and woman——"* Here there may have been a shrug of the graceful shoulders. *"There would be no danger from them, for they babble like children and no one would believe them. But they must die, too, along with the girl, for they would only be burdens, useless."*

——*"Where, Cieta? Where would be the best place?"*

——*"You will find someplace on the road. Away from the house so that their bodies will not be discovered for a long time. Perhaps in the woods while you are pretending to go away with them."*

I could see it all with such vividness and hear it so clearly in my mind that I closed my

199

eyes and threw my hands up over my ears. But I could not shut out the fact of Craig there with the knife blade held only inches away from me.

My voice sounded muffled as I cried out, "The shoes!"

The freshly-polished shoes which had influenced me in my decision to ask Craig to go with us! He had not been a prisoner in his room as I had thought. If he had managed to make his way downstairs tonight, he could have done the same thing before.

The figure I had seen digging in the grave-yard had looked small when I had seen it from the roof. And I had attributed that to distance. But I knew now that it had been Craig who had been there. Small as he was, it would not have been a difficult matter for him to have hidden behind one of the tombstones. Because he was shorter than I, his hitting me with something, a stick, a piece of branch, had not had such a serious effect as it would have had we been the same height.

And the shoes.... Grown muddy in the cemetery, they had been cleaned and polished.

He was raging at me now because I had not obeyed his commands quickly enough. "Get the others out, like I told you," and he pushed me toward the back of the wagon.

I wanted to rebel, having no wish to be a party to the dreadful fate in store for Grandfather and Aunt Charlotte, but I knew it would be useless. And then Craig seized my arm with his free hand and twisted it until I cried out in pain. He screamed at the other two to get out of the cart and rather than run the risk of having them fall, I stretched out my hands to help them when Craig had released me. Although what could broken old bones have mattered then when we were all to die soon?

Craig! I slid a glance in his direction, unable to believe that this harsh-voiced cripple with murder in his heart was the quiet boy who had lain so patiently in bed. And when I remembered him like that, I saw in my mind the papers and marine charts that had littered the coverlet.

Why had I not suspected before? Known that Craig did not lie there day after day with nothing to occupy him except his books and games? He had been engaged in a far more deadly game. He had been Cieta's confederate in crime. It was he who charted the course of the ships which came bearing their cargoes of human misery. He had been an important participant in the evil that went on at Blacktower.

My heart yearned toward the two old people who stood beside me on the dark road. Grandfather still seemed lost and unaware, but Aunt Charlotte had evidently been shocked back into reality. She was staring at Craig with eyes that were filled with pain. There was heartbreak in her voice when she cried out, "Oh, my poor boy, she has won completely! She has taken your soul and given it to the Devil! I would not believe it was this bad. I had hoped——I had hoped——"

His face seemed to quaver for a moment and I searched it looking for signs of weakening. What she had said had struck him, but not in the way I had hoped. The maniacal smile was back and he sneered through it, "Your little homeless waif didn't turn out the way you hoped, did he? You expected a pet dog who would lie at your feet and lick your hand. Oh, you did your duty, dear Aunt Charlotte! You took me in because there was no one else to do it. Probably you expect stars in your crown for your generosity. But that's all it was——duty! You never loved me. Who could love an ugly wreck like me? Only Cieta!"

So that was how it had been. A crippled boy chafing under the fact that he was an object of charity. Aunt Charlotte was sensitive and un-used to the ugliness of the world. Once, a long time ago perhaps, she might have winced at the sight of Craig's twisted legs. That would have assumed too great importance in his mind. With long, dreary hours to brood in, he might have let kindle inside him a hatred for the world that had used him cruelly.

He had only Cieta to turn to, Cieta who was a stranger in the cold, big house. No doubt she, too, had been starved for love, rejected by her father as she had been, and had given all her own love to the only boy available. He had been young, younger than she, but he had been at Blacktower only through sufferance, too, and he needed her. I had known about his dependence on her. But I didn't know its extent nor the method she had used to enslave him until Aunt Charlotte suddenly burst into tears and began to babble through her sobs.

"....I am not as stupid as you think....I have known for a long time.... It is the floranoctine.... She gives it to you as a reward, withholds it as a punishment...."

I heard no more of what she was saying. The word "floranoctine" was clamoring in my brain. Only a little while ago, in one of the Boston papers, I had read about the drug that had been called "worse than opium, the scourge of the tropical countries." Fruit of the floranocta, "nightflower," its leaves were ground for a drug so addicting and crime-producing that it was outlawed in all civilized countries. And this is what Cieta had been feeding to Craig!

For a moment or two, while the knowledge swept over me, I was numb with the awfulness of it. Then feeling came back to me gradually. I remembered the sweetish smell of Craig's bedroom, his different and quickly-changing moods. So this was Cieta's whip. No doubt she had withheld the drug from him all day and would reward him with it when he had disposed of us. Even now I thought I could see the signs of his craving of it. His face began to twitch and there was a faint desperation on it and a film of moisture over his eyes.

I could not pity him in that moment knowing, as I did, that the ghost-like ships which had slipped into the waters beyond Blacktower carried something even more terrible than unhappy human beings. For from what other source could Cieta obtain the drug that kept Craig prisoner? And I realized that it was not his love for her that held him to her but his craving for floranoctine.

The torture of that craving might be beginning, but his wits were still clear, his hand steady on the knife. It would be only moments now. And then Prince, the big dog who had fallen asleep in the back seat and been forgotten by all of us, stirred and barked. I cried out to him, "Prince! Come here!" in a desperate hope that there might be some help from that quarter.

He came bounding over the wagon and threw himself in front of me. I screamed, "Sic him, Prince! He is planning to do us harm!"

The dog evidently had no notion of what I wanted him to do. Wherever he belonged, it was only too plain that he had never been a watchdog. This might be the reason he was roaming around homeless. Perhaps he had been turned out by his owner because of his uselessness.

He sat crouched down on his paws, his tail wagging and his eyes bright with expectancy while he waited for me to tell him how to proceed in the game. I waved my arms and cried, "Siç him!" again and Prince got up and ambled slowly in Craig's direction.

The whole thing would be farcical under any other circumstances and I had a wild, hysterical impulse to laugh. The laugh died in my throat when Craig, whose body seemed to become a shuddering, twitching thing, saw the dog coming toward him and aimed a foot at its nose.

Prince barked happily and dashed at the uplifted leg. Small as it was, a long portion of it disappeared in the dog's mouth. He shook it with a playful growl and Craig's arms flailed out as he tried to hold his balance. There was that moment when he looked as though he were performing a strange sort of solo dance. Then he went over backwards and the knife shot out of his hand.

I could have escaped then. The woods were behind me and I might have dashed into them. Crippled as he was, Craig could not have overtaken me for he was scrambling around on the ground still for his knife and fear would have sped my footsteps into and through the deep forest.

But there would be no escape for Grandfather and Aunt Charlotte. I could not leave them to the mercy of a man whose craving was making him furious. I had to stay and watch him, fascinated and frozen as a bird staring into the eyes of a snake, as he pulled himself up by grasping the side of the wagon and then came toward me again with the knife in his hand.

His face was twisted with rage and hatred because we were delaying his return to Cieta and the drug that awaited him. He would waste no more time. The knife blade was no brighter than his eyes. Then it became lost to my view because he was pressing it against my throat.

I heard Aunt Charlotte cry out and from the corner of my eye I saw her gather up her skirts and try to run around the corner of the wagon in the direction of the road. But she had gone only a few steps before I heard the thud of her body against the ground and I knew that she had fallen.

She lay there wailing and the sound of her voice was dirge-like, an elegy for all of us who must die in this lonely spot.

I thought I heard another sound cutting through her wailing, a sound which became louder as my brain whirled in turmoil. It could not be real. My imagination, in that moment of frenzied terror, must be playing tricks on me. But still it seemed to approach, that noise of galloping hoofs until the air was filled with it.

And then I saw the shadowy outlines of a carriage coming around the bend in the road and bearing down on us. Craig dropped his hand and whirled, his face awful in that moment of recognition.

The lights of the carriage flooded over us and we were like figures in a tableau. I was the first to move. I ran to throw myself over Aunt Charlotte who lay in the path of the galloping horse. It pulled up before it was upon us and I looked up and saw that there were three men in the carriage.

As I got up slowly from the ground, I heard a loud, animal-like cry tear from Craig's throat. I turned my head as he was plunging in the direction of the woods, one leg dragging behind him and the other making its strange lifting motion.

A man jumped from the carriage and ran after him. Another came to Aunt Charlotte's side and lifted her to her feet. The third——.

I saw Dr. Andrew Bruce come running into the pool of light around the wagon. I murmured his name and I tried to remain standing upright until he reached me. But my body seemed to have become a mass of soft, gelatinous substance and I slid to the ground. I felt the earth against my face and then oblivion overwhelmed me.

CHAPTER FIFTEEN

The cold night air revived me and strong arms——Andrew's——lifted me into the carriage. My wits returned and I was no worse for the swooning, but I let him hold me close with one arm while he held the reins with his other hand. The feeling of his coat was warm against my cheek and a safe, comforting euphoria began to spread over me.

Grandfather and Aunt Charlotte were in the back seat and I heard her murmur something to him soothingly. The horrible thing she had revealed came surging into my mind for an instant; but I closed it out deliberately, not wanting this wonderful interlude of closeness with Andrew to be destroyed.

I did not even wonder how he had happened to come upon us there on the dark road nor about the identity of the two men who rode with Craig in the wagon ahead of us. Of course he had not been able to escape. His plunge into the woods had been futile; his poor twisted legs had precluded speed and the men overtook him, it seemed, before he had gone more than a few feet. While I had been coming out of the fainting spell, I had heard the stern voices of the two men and Craig's whimpering.

The gates of Blacktower were still open and we followed the wagon through them. As we approached the house, I pulled away from Andrew's encircling arm and sat up. Now I must face it all again. I pressed my hands together to keep from shivering and he turned to look at me with concern.

"It will soon be over."

"Not too soon for me. Who are they?" I asked. "The men who rescued us? Are they the police?"

One, he told me, was a government man, the other the sheriff of the county. "For a long time now——"

Then he broke off, for the wagon had stopped at the foot of the entrance steps. He tossed the reins over the horse's back and leaped out. As I waited for him to help Grandfather and Aunt Charlotte out of the carriage, I stood looking at the three men grouped at the door. They appeared ghostly in the fog, which seemed to have whitened and thickened even during our short absence.

The taller of the two men held Craig, and as we joined them, he said to Andrew, "I am sure there will be no trouble. When she sees that we have this one, she will probably go to pieces. But the sheriff has a gun, just in case."

So this was the government man. I had never seen him before in my life, yet because of him we were alive. I would have guessed from his air of authority, I think, that he was the one who was in charge. At any rate he motioned for the sheriff to gain entrance for us and we stood silently waiting. The door was locked, of course, and so there was a delay while the sheriff pounded the knocker up and down several times.

Seconds stretched into minutes. The sound of the knocker shattered the stillness of the night again and again. And then, finally, the door swung open and Cieta stood there, her figure silhouetted against the light in back of her. I could not see her face, but I could not have missed the confident, almost triumphant movement of her arms, the expectancy with which she had been prepared to meet Craig and only Craig.

The sight of us all there froze her into immobility for several long moments and then, with her hand still on the door, she tried to close us out. The government man was too quick for her. He shoved himself through the opening. When she fell back and moved along the hall, her eyes still on his face, he followed her and then overtook her.

By the time I had drawn up behind the others in front of me, she was held there by the vise of his hand on her arm. She looked away from him, her eyes went to Craig's face and there was black fire in them. On her face was a look of shattered agony.

I had to turn my own eyes away. It was not pity which made the naked pain impossible for me to look on. I could feel no compassion for this woman who had used human beings to satisfy her greed. But I knew I was seeing Cieta's very heart. And I sensed that it was breaking into little pieces at the sight of Craig held captive.

She could never have known love in its real form and so would not have been aware of its tender aspects. Product of a marriage which never should have been, she must have inherited the quality of greed from both her parents——Captain Lawson, who had not cared by what method he obtained gold, and the island girl who had married a man fifty years older than she for what other reason except that he was wealthy?

Undoubtedly Cieta had come to realize that Craig would never love her as she loved him but was only dependent on her for attention; this must be the reason she had contrived to foster his need to even greater lengths. I could guess that she had fed the drug to him gradually at first to alleviate his mental suffering because he would never be able to be like other boys and to sooth the chafing of being an object of charity. She had helped him to escape into a false world, binding him more and more closely to her as he needed larger and more frequent doses of the floranoctine.

He was crying out now. "Cieta, I tried! Oh, Cieta, I did try! But they came before I could do it!"

In her rage and hurt, she spat out at him. "Be quiet! You have spoiled everything! Well, you will suffer for it, too. For it was you as well. I could have not done it all alone with only that stupid donkey, Julio——!"

She regained her control and drew her body up into a stiff, defiant stance as she turned to the government man. "You will find it hard to prove any sort of wrongdoing, Senor. I have merely been befriending a few of my poor, unfortunate countrymen."

He snorted a laugh. "You are over-optimistic, young woman. When the evidence is all in, when we search the house and open up the graves out yonder, you may sing a different song."

I did not wait while they went into the tower, because Andrew said to me, "You had better get the two old people to bed. I'm afraid this has been too much for them both."

He came with me to the second floor. We left Aunt Charlotte in her room and first gave our attention to Grandfather who seemed to need it most. When I had him undressed and settled in his bed, Andrew gave him a pill from the bottle he had left with me. We left the lamp burning in case the remembered terrors of the night came back to disturb him. Then we went along the hall to reassure Aunt Charlotte as best we could.

I had calming words all ready in my mind, but when we opened her door we found that she had changed from the clothing she had worn and was back in her nightgown. She was in bed and seemed, incredibly, to be already asleep. I stood looking down at her for a moment, not too much worried for I felt that there was hope for Aunt Charlotte. What she had called "the curse of the Lawsons" could not have her too firmly in its grip as yet. Grandfather? I did not know. We would have to wait and see.

"We". Andrew and I, of course. I had accepted, without conscious thought, our being together. Yet there had not been a personal word between us since he had leaped out of the carriage and run to my side. His holding me close to him as we had driven back to Blacktower might have been only a sympathetic response to my need for comforting.

Shyness made me draw away from him as we went down the staircase. And we were silent when we came into the stillness of the front hall. The others were gone now. I had not heard the carriage nor the wagon pulling out of the lane but I guessed that Cieta and Craig had been taken away and, if there had been room for them, some of the people in the tower.

Andrew said at last, "We had better get some coffee into you. You're probably still shaking inside and it was a raw night to be out there."

"I'm afraid it would keep me from sleeping."

It was an inane remark. Of course I wouldn't be able to sleep, coffee or not, while there were still questions unanswered. The most important one clamored in my brain until I could not help asking it.

"How did you happen to come along at just the right moment?"

He said, "First things first. The kitchen is back this way, isn't it?" He took my arm and led me down the hall. He found matches and lit the gas globes in the kitchen. I sat by lethargically while he rummaged in the pantry for the canister of coffee, a measuring spoon and a pair of cups and saucers.

"I'm a good cook, you know. I had to learn to be since I have no wife to do for me."

As the coffee began to bubble, the smell of it filled the room and I realized how hungry I was, how many hours had passed since I had eaten anything at all. He seemed to guess that for he took a skillet down from its peg on the wall and eggs and bacon from the icebox.

Bacon and eggs and coffee——there was nothing about this, our first meal together, that even suggested romance. Yet when I looked up at him across the table from time to time, I knew such happiness as I had never known before. I wished that it could last forever, this feeling of intimacy here in the kitchen, when the silence was as comfortable and right as though we had been doing this very thing for many years.

The silence was one which he had imposed upon me, refusing to let me speak until we had finished eating. Then he leaned back in his chair and said, "Fire away!"

But now I was not so much concerned with the answers he would give me to my questions as the fact that everything must be clean and honest between us. Much as I hated what I had to say——and at first the words seemed to stick in my throat——I knew that it must be done.

"Andrew, I have misjudged you so! But I did not know what to think of you. When you made love to me, your mind was on Cieta."

He demanded, "You did not really believe that!"

"I did, indeed. Because you spoke of her immediately after——after you held me in your arms. I thought it was Cieta you loved. And then I found you in the cemetery and I ——I believed that you had been with her. For a long time. Perhaps——perhaps for the entire night."

My voice petered out, for I expected that he would grow angry over what I had said. But he only laughed and said, on an indulgent note, "Little idiot! Cieta was never anything to me except an object of suspicion. I became involved in this thing because Foster——he's the government agent, by the way——sought me out and asked me to help him. There were things——well, a body had been found in the woods and several others on the north road. And there was evidence that a certain illegal drug was being smuggled over the Canadian border. The ships, the ones that brought it in along with the people who were smuggled in, too, have been sighted a couple of times but there were no records that they had ever reached any port.

"The authorities have been suspicious of this place for a long time. When Foster asked for my help, I felt it my duty as a citizen to give it to him. I'd heard the stories myself, of course, from time to time. About a wagon full of people going through Seamount late at night; strangers on the road; a boy here in Blacktower that no one ever saw from the time he arrived here.

"Foster's idea was that a doctor, seeing people all the time and going from house to house on sick calls, would be in a position to find out things without arousing suspicion. I tried to think of excuses for looking this place over. Yesterday morning I was a few miles beyond this place——I'd been called out for a birth during the night. When I was on my way past, I decided to do a little detecting. That time of day——well, I thought I'd be safe. I'd heard about the cemetery but never seen it. I didn't know what excuse I'd make for being there if Cieta or the man who runs her errands had found me. But of course I saw no one, only you. I thought for a moment when I saw you lying there that someone had killed you."

His voice had grown hoarse and he stretched out his hand and gripped mine. Then he got up and came around the table. He put his fingers gently on the back of my head.

"No bad effects?"

"None. Oh, Andrew!"

There were so many things I wanted to tell him, to say that I was sorry, shamed by my suspicions. I clung to his hand and I would have spoken then but he was still talking about what had happened in the graveyard.

"You were attacked, weren't you? I knew from the first moment that it was no fall such as you had described to me."

"I lied, Andrew, because I was not sure about you. It was Craig, I am sure, who struck me down."

"Craig! But I thought——"

"It couldn't have been anybody else. Julio was scared to death of the graveyard. And it was a man's figure I saw from the roof that morning, a short man."

Then I told him my theory of Craig using a stick lying close at hand, or a stone he picked up, and aiming it at my head. And that the blow had not been more effective than it was because of his shortness.

"Perhaps he was trying to be a hero in her eyes then, as he did later, so that she would reward him with more of the drug. I don't

217

know. But it was Cieta the first time. She was the one who tried to smother me with a pillow the first night we arrived."

His face was very white and still. "I knew nothing about that."

"They pretended it never happened, told me that I was dreaming, both Aunt Charlotte and Cieta. Because of course it was when Cieta had Grandfather's sister completely in her power. Later, when her brother proved to be sick and likely to die, Aunt Charlotte made a stand. Cieta must have seen that there were limits beyond which she couldn't go. But then——" and I shuddered at the memory.

He made me tell him the whole story and I finished, "I realized that it was a woman. I saw that much. Besides, if it had been Craig then, he undoubtedly would have been able to kill me. His arms were strong——I saw the way he drove the horse. It was only his lack of stature that defeated him in the graveyard."

"Alicia! Alicia!" He came around the table and drew me to my feet. "If I had lost you!"

I wanted to stay there close to him and close my mind to all the horror-filled things, but I knew they would never be completely exorcised until everything was said. "The graveyard is full of all those who died or were killed by Cieta. That's why she wanted Craig to take us away and murder us where our bodies wouldn't be found——I'm sure that is the truth. I know, too, why Aunt Charlotte was

218

so shattered on the night that we came here. She was terrified that we would discover what Cieta was doing and she did not want us to know that Craig was here because we might have learned about the drug. She tried to protect her father's memory. It was always that.

"If she had known that we were coming, she would have written back, I'm sure, with some excuse to keep us from Blacktower. But Cieta evidently destroyed the letter as she must have destroyed all correspondence that came to the house because she wanted no one in it to have any link with the outside world. But why?" I asked. "In this case why would she keep that letter away from Aunt Charlotte when she doubtlessly could have prevailed upon her to write to us and tell us not to come?"

And then, suddenly, I had the answer to my own question.

"Cieta," I said slowly, "probably does not know how to read or write. Aunt Charlotte told me that she was the one who had taught Craig his lessons. If Cieta had any education at all, she would have taken over the teaching as she took over everything else in his life. I wonder that she even allowed him his books. Although, of course, he was twelve when he came and his education had already begun. That must have been the way it was. For it was Craig who was in touch with the men who sailed Cieta's ships and charted the courses. That fell to him since she was unable to do those things. And Craig must have, first of all, read Captain Lawson's log and told Cieta who she was."

I was shaken by what I had deduced. Cieta had brought on her own doom, started the chain of events which led to her capture by destroying Grandfather's letter. Perhaps she had been able to distinguish postmarks and burned and tore up all those she recognized as not coming from one of the men who were her confederates. Through such a simple circumstance, she had met her fate.

"Enough!" Andrew sounded stern and masterful. "You've talked about it enough now. Tomorrow we will get you away. I know of doctors in Boston who may be able to help Mrs. Prescott and your grandfather. I will give you letters to them."

"I shall be going away. And you will stay here, Andrew!"

"You do not believe that we will never see each other again?" He put a hand under my chin and lifted it so that I was forced to look into his face. I tried to pull away for I did not want him to see the tears that had flooded my eyes when he had spoken of my going away. For a moment everything was blurred and shattered in my vision and then he drew me close into his embrace and my damp cheek was against his jaw.

I moved until my mouth was almost on his

and I was the one who said it. "I love you, I love you," I murmured.

It did not matter who said it first. Because I knew. I knew in my heart, suddenly grown joyous, that there was no greater love nor lesser degree of love between us. His kiss told me and my pulses raced as it demanded a return of his own ardor.

I was shaken by the time I stepped away from him. "You have had no sleep tonight, Andrew. And there are people who need you. And I—well, I must see to Grandfather and Aunt Charlotte. And there is packing to do."

Such mundane things these were to keep us apart. But it would be only for a little while, he promised. He said that he would be back as soon as possible.

I walked to the door with him. I reminded him that there was no means of transportation to take him back to Seamount. He replied that he would go out into the road and hitch a ride from anyone who was passing in a carriage or a farm wagon.

"It is light now and there will be people abroad on their way to the village."

I saw with surprise that it *was* light. When he threw open the door, there were no mists to greet us and the sky was streaked with the pale colors of dawn. The long, dark night had ended.

We stood there for a moment, Andrew and I, with our arms around each other. The scattering of the fog was a symbol of what lay ahead for us. The dawn was a promise. And Blacktower——the big house that rose at our backs——was, in all respects, behind us. Its terrors had fled with the new day.

DENISE ROBINS

"Rarely has a writer of our times delved so deeply into the secret places of a woman's heart."

—Taylor Caldwell

☐ **ALL THAT MATTERS.** He needed a glamor girl to further his career, but all she wanted to be was his wife. Could shy, retiring Glynis, with her hand-made clothes and simple ideals, be any match for the other women in his life?

☐ **A LOVE LIKE OURS.** Was she just a passing fancy, or did she mean more than that to him? But their love would be hopeless in any case. She was just the green-eyed daughter of an old friend, and he was the world's most eligible bachelor.

☐ **THE NOBLE ONE.** Diana's special qualities attracted two very different men. Brett considered her a friend who shared his enthusiasm for the outdoor life. But Keith, wealthy and spoiled, wanted to possess her and to change her. . . .

☐ **REPUTATION.** Vivian had nearly ruined Lucinda's life before, with her unreasonable jealousy and terrible accusations. Now that Lucinda was engaged to another man, would Vivian let the past rest?

☐ **GAY DEFEAT.** With her father's ruin, spoiled Delia abruptly ceased to dance her way through life. To Martin, her father's lawyer, Delia was a helpless—almost useless—member of society who needed protecting. So he offered to marry her.

☐ **HOUSE OF THE SEVENTH CROSS.** She awoke as a prisoner in a strange house and with an unfamiliar identity. But though her memory had been shattered, she still had the strength to love. . . .

** only 75¢ each **

GREAT GOTHICS

Big in size, scope, and supersettings—
fantastic Gothic reading from popular
authors

WHISPER OF FEAR, Elna Stone
She heard her mother whispering in the night—only
her mother was dead. . . .

THE DARK WING, June Wetherell
A young girl with a shameful secret finds herself in a
house of strangers—only to discover they have secrets
of their own.

THE WATCHER IN THE DARK, Angela Gray
Real or phantom . . . ? She only knew that each time
the apparition appeared, disaster struck. . . .

MOSSHAVEN, Sibyl Hancock
A cryptic clue sent Stephanie in search of her mother's
relatives—even though she'd been warned to stay away.

MASTER OF FOXHOLLOW, Susan Claudia
The offer of a home for Christy and her fatherless children was a godsend—until she found out *which god*
had sent it. . . .